WELCOME TO KWEENDOM

LGBTQ Comedians Make Pride Personal with Stories of
Love, Loss, Sex, and Everything Under The Rainbow

Edited by Bobby Hankinson

Welcome to Kweendom:
LGBTQ Comedians Make Pride Personal with Stories of Love,
Loss, Sex, and Everything Under The Rainbow

First paperback edition 2021

ISBN 978-1-7335682-6-5 (paperback)

Library of Congress Control Number: 2020947853

Published by Wheatfield Press, LLC
www.wheatfieldpress.com

Dedicated to the fearless queer community.

Table of Contents

Foreword

When I was a drama student, one of the first things my movement teacher said that registered with me — actually, hang on, it might be the only thing my movement teacher said that ever registered with me — was: "Everyone should go to drama school, not just people who want to be actors, but everyone. Here, you learn about life!"

I feel the same way about this collection of short stories. Of course, it is much more likely that queer people (and by that I mean all the letters of our beautiful and ever expanding acronym AND those who love them) will be reading this book than non-queer people, but I so wish that our tired, eager to compartmentalize and label "oh, that's not for me," throw-them-a-bone culture would wise up and realize that queer people have got it down. If wisdom means having experienced life in its many and varied forms, taken that experience and analyzed it, then used that analysis to go forth into the world with a new, stronger and more authentic outlook, then this book will testify, teach and preach, that queer people, per capita, are much more likely to be wise than the rest of the poor unfortunate non-queer folks.

This anthology is as eclectic as it is possible to be. One dip into its lucky bag might present you with a tender story of navigating the world of Judaism as a trans person, then another will give you an insight on the intricate rules and etiquette of piss play.

The revenge fantasy of returning to interview for a job as a woman that you were once fired from as a man competes with the joyous abandon yet utterly overwhelming (and ultimately rather tawdry) experience of being blindfolded and losing count of the number of times you are fucked in a Berlin sex club.

There is even a story about dog death that is haunting and hilarious and many queer insights into topics ranging from the Vietnamese-American community to eating disorders to alcoholic parents to having an impenetrable anxiety about being, er, penetrated.

What this collection makes transparent is that all of us, as queer people, have a secret that we may have lived with for a very long time. And even if we haven't, we can all appreciate the concept of hiding some detail of ourselves. Every storyteller in these pages has some form of secret or encounters one. What is illuminating and remarkable and heartening is how they deal with it.

The common theme in all of these wonderful stories is authenticity and, eventually, lack of shame. My biggest takeaway, and something I think we should all heed, is that we should never respect anyone who shows us no respect — even when they are dominating or humiliating us. And that living an authentic life, whatever that may mean to you, is paramount in life because it will give us the liberty to pursue true happiness.

—Alan Cumming

Preface

People ask, "When did you know you were queer?" and it's never an easy question to answer. Maybe it was when I was in kindergarten and desperately wanted to hold hands with my best friend. Maybe it was all the times I was wishing I was doing anything other than team sports. Or maybe it was when Grace Jones popped out of a box and sang "Little Drummer Boy" on the *Pee-Wee's Playhouse Christmas Special.*

Who can say?

But one memory that sticks with me is much more mundane. I remember laying in the top bunk of my bunk bed, inches from the ceiling, staring up into the dark, envisioning my future and seeing ... nothing.

Not tragedy, not hardship, but literally nothing. Emptiness. A void. File not found. I had never met an openly queer person. I didn't even know where to look. As far as I knew, there were no other options. There was no future.

I was 9.

Into my teenage years, I made friends, I found art, I even had one of those totally-wrong-for-you boyfriends you pick up when you're a gay teen in the suburbs, thanks in equal part to scarcity and desperation. I was this pseudo-punk, feminist, writer-type, and he was a huge sports fan, attended monster truck rallies without irony and once entered AND WON a contest to introduce his favorite band — SMASH MOUTH — live on stage in Vegas.

We dated for 2.5 years.

It's not that I was some prize. I was this sort of a surly, schlumpy, suburban closet case, skulking around in big, black, baggy clothes. I was like a teenage Gargamel from *The Smurfs*. That was my aesthetic. I kept my homosexuality a secret from my parents using this great trick where I just never came home. You need to remember, this was two years before the original *Queer Eye* and eight years ahead of *Glee*. This was back when no one bothered to tell gay teens it got better, because lots of folks weren't convinced that was the case yet.

Spurred on by fiery female punk bands and my ragtag group of whip-smart weirdo friends, I began to embrace parts of my identity, even if it was not always as openly as I would have liked. After my parents read my perfectly banal college admissions essay, for example, I snuck down to the family computer to add a part about helping start the gay-straight alliance in my high school before submitting.

It was the tiniest taste of embracing my identity, but it was enough to get me to commit to starting college as my full, authentic self. It was thrilling. I finally felt like I had access to all the parts of my brain that had been previously dedicated solely to keeping secrets or wasting energy trying to fit my very queer existence into these uncomfortable frameworks. No more. If there was no future, well, there would be nothing to lose.

Every day that passed without the sky falling (and even on days when it did a little bit) I became more and more untethered from the fear of my queerness. In a lot of ways, it started to feel like a superpower. Was it exhausting keeping secrets, always reading the room, needing to instantly assess if the person I was interacting with was safe to let my guard down? Sure. But it also honed my intuition and empathy.

Turns out, those same skills could also detect if someone needed help or a smile or, sometimes, the very thing someone is trying to say but just doesn't know how.

I was free to engineer whatever life felt right for me. And that's not just good for queer people; it helps change things for even the cisgender, straight folks out there who feel trapped, too. It's like getting a LEGO set, and instead of building the submarine or whatever's on the box, you use the pieces to make a unicorn or a cyborg or the Christmas scene from John Waters' *Female Trouble*. The possibilities are endless.

Some might argue that all this fear and worry and trauma makes queer people "sensitive," as if that's a pejorative. It's not a weakness to feel things more deeply. That sensitivity is what makes a song or a picture or a scene in a film that much more beautiful. (Oh, you thought it was just a coincidence the way the queer community reacts to performers like Judy, Barbra and even Carly Rae Jepsen?)

I soon started writing about LGBTQ topics for the school paper, the local magazine, the Boston Globe, the Houston Chronicle, and more. I began writing for a large, national LGBTQ news website, and, despite all warnings, I ventured into the comments section. There was a lot of ugly, a lot of hurt, a lot Dorito-dusted, hateful internet goblins. But even in disagreements, I noticed something special. This was a community, and for some queer people across the world, this was the only community they had.

I was still finding my own community when I moved to New York and started performing comedy. I met countless hilarious, queer performers and began appearing on lineups for LGBTQ-themed shows around the city. Often, these shows were mostly cis, white, gay men with a few "cool" straight girls thrown in the mix.

Thus, Kweendom was born. It started as a challenge: prove there are enough diverse, talented, queer people to support an ongoing show without allies. As I often say at the top of the show: Allies are great, thank you for your service, I just think queer people make better art, don't @ me.

Now, nearly five years later, this scrappy, little show has hosted hundreds of queer comedians from around the world. Some have gone on to *SNL*, late night, and more. We've toured other cities. The queer comedy scene is booming, and there are more queer shows — and more diverse queer shows — every day.

So, when the opportunity to put together a Kweendom book was presented, I knew it had to be a reflection of not just the show, but this incredible community.

I don't know what exactly I was expecting when I asked a bunch of comedians to write essays about queerness, but it certainly wasn't the vulnerable, thrilling, heartbreaking, hopeful, and powerful pieces I received. They were funny, sure, but they were so much more.

As unique as each story was, there were themes, motifs and even details that kept re-emerging. There were moments where someone's experience spoke so deeply, so strongly to my own, I had to put down my laptop and walk away.

Because even today, with all the apps, social media, and record-level representation, it's still just as easy as ever to feel isolated and alone. There are just as many ways to be queer as there are queer people, and there is always going to be someone else staring up at the ceiling, waiting to see their future.

You're not going to relate to every essay here, and that's OK! Some things might not resonate with you today, but in three months, it could be just the thing. Take what you need. The rest will be waiting.

To help navigate, we've loosely grouped the essays by theme. This is just one way any of these multidimensional essays could be classified; you may find yourself piecing together your own sort of Kweendom director's cut of your favorites across topics to turn to when you need to feel understood, expand your thinking, or just have a laugh.

We took inspiration for our topics from the rainbow Pride flag. Designed by Gilbert Baker, each stripe on the Pride flag has a meaning: red for life, orange for healing, yellow for sunlight, green for nature, blue for harmony, and purple for spirit. We have our own interpretations of these themes, which will be introduced before each chapter of essays.

Most importantly, the rainbow is a symbol of unity, beautiful parts coming together to make an even more magical whole. Our community is stronger because of — not in spite of — all the things that make us unique. No matter where you are, you're part of this now. You belong here.

So, welcome to Kweendom, where everybody is welcome. And everybody rules.

Deciding how to interpret "life" wasn't easy. Life is all-encompassing. Life is beautiful. Life is a mystery, everyone must stand alone. OK, that's Madonna, but still, it applies.

For queer people, life is survival. So, it seems a little ironic that we begin with a few stories about death — deaths of loved ones, deaths of past lives, deaths of dreams.

But even in death there are new beginnings. The LGBTQ community knows that maybe more than most. And like our forebearers spun tragedy into art and resistance, these first writers look unflinchingly at loss and find whatever there is to gain.

FATHER AND SON

by Calvin Cato

It was spring of 2015 in New York City. I was in a doctor's office with my dad, and the doctor said, "Your liver cancer is advancing, and we need to discuss options."

Most people would think "cancer" is the scariest word in that sentence, but for me it was "options." My dad had been living with liver cancer for a year and a half, but if you looked at him you wouldn't have been able to tell. He ate his vegetables, he didn't smoke, he quit drinking. Hell, he didn't even wear glasses.

Yet there we were, in a windowless room listening to the doctor present "options," like a waiter telling us tonight's house specials. 'For an appetizer, we recommend some life changes. For a main course, we offer surgery, liver transplantation, chemotherapy, or radiation.' Surgery was out of the question because the doctor worried about my dad's ability to survive it. A transplant would be difficult because it required waiting on a long list. I sat with my fingers laced together and deferred to my dad, who worked as a registered nurse.

After we decided on a combination of radiation and chemotherapy, the doctor told us the full details. For five weeks, Monday through Friday, my dad would receive three hour-long chemotherapy treatments. The doctor peered at me over his bifocals. "You will have to arrive at the clinic by 9 a.m. every day. Do you think you'll be up to the task?"

I jolted in my seat; I didn't know it was my turn to speak. "Yes, of course I can."

But could I? Taking care of my dad would involve three things I hate: waking up early, driving in New York City, and spending six uninterrupted hours with my father.

My dad and I were complete opposites. He was an immigrant who believed that dreams are things you forget about as soon as you wake up. I was a knockabout standup comic. My dad believed in schedules; I worshipped procrastination. Before his diagnosis, the longest conversation we had was an explosive argument when I was 23 about why I would throw my education away to pursue a career in entertainment.

"You could be a doctor. You can *still* be a doctor!" he fumed.

Nevertheless, I committed to Driving Mr. Daisy. I renewed my driver's license, and despite some near collisions, got the hang of bobbing and weaving through streets clogged with cab drivers and bicyclists. I bought Red Bull by the truckload to keep myself awake and aware. I even practiced talking to my dad by writing conversation topics on index cards and staging fake dialogue.

On day one, there was palpable silence. I was more like an Uber driver trying to earn a five-star rating than a son. Day two was somehow worse, because the silence was replaced by my dad monologuing about my terrible driving. "Why are you driving too slow? Why didn't you cut that guy off? Why *did* you cut *that* guy off? Are you even listening to me?" I briefly debated tucking and rolling out of the car, but that would have been rude.

Because my ex-boyfriend was a radio DJ (but *not* a shock jock, I have at least some self-respect), I had nearly 100 CDs to choose from in my car. Only four made it into heavy rotation: Earth, Wind & Fire (one of the major architects of the black pop sound), Tom Petty (a classic rock and roll artist), The Fugees (a must-have for any fans of '90s R&B and hip-hop) and … Eminem. Yes, that angry bleach-blond white rapper, with songs about killing his mother and ex-girlfriend.

"That white boy is crazy," my dad would say, humming along to Eminem's fantasy murder sprees.

At the end of the week, we were driving home from chemotherapy, making stilted small talk. I got distracted, made a wrong turn, and we ended up on the way to Coney Island, less of a beach comprised of sand than Band-Aids and broken glass.

"Why'd you get off at this exit?" my dad asked.

"I don't know, Dad." I braced myself for an onslaught of unhelpful advice.

"Well, I'm a bit hungry. Wanna go to Nathan's while we're here?"

Nathan's was one of our traditions when I was a kid. We'd buy hot dogs and cheese fries and walk along the boardwalk.

"I will, if you're paying."

Don't think I'm callous; I'm just unemployed, and most of my money was going to gas and energy drinks.

The day was undeniably beautiful and, because beach season hadn't started yet, the boardwalk was empty. We finished our artery-clogging meal and began our walk.

"So, how's your stand-up comedy going?" he asked.

I was shocked. My dad had never shown interest in my career. "It's going alright. I'm doing a lot of shows, but I feel like I may be stalling out."

"You know, you should try to talk to Steve Harvey, I'm sure he can help you."

"That's not exactly how comedy works."

My father shot me a pained expression.

"You know, I'll look into that," I said out of guilt. "How do you feel, being the patient instead of the nurse?"

"I don't really like it. I hate needles and all the tests."

"What was the craziest thing you had to do as a nurse?"

"Well, I saw so many things. One time I had to help a cop who was attacked by some guy. He was stabbed, and I had to help get the knife out and stuff."

"And stuff?! That's pretty incredible."

"Eh. I mean, he lived."

I couldn't believe how nonchalant he was about the whole thing.

"How about you? What kind of shows have you been doing?"

I told him about a rough show I did once in a conservative Midwest suburb whose name corresponds with an obscure racial slur. The place was in a glorified cowboy saloon without a proper stage, and the closest thing to a minority I saw was a young white woman with dreadlocks. I performed for 10 minutes to abject silence and ended up getting paid partially in change.

"That's not what I expected," my dad said after a pause.

Maybe he was onto something about calling Steve Harvey.

The next week, I made more concerted travel plans. I started our series of road trips by going to Rockaway Beach, where we used to get ice cream and ride bicycles. On another trip, we drove to my late grandfather's old house and tooled around the neighborhood. We got to my dad's old co-worker's house, and I listened to them share emergency room war stories. If my dad felt strong enough to walk, we'd stroll about. On days when he felt tired, we just sat somewhere. And on days when he was too weak to stand, we'd just drive and reminisce. Not every conversation was pleasant, but even the more tense talks didn't end with the one-two punch of our typical temper tantrum and silent treatment.

Still, I had one final challenge to face: coming out to my dad. I'm sure he suspected, but I never said the words. For most of my life, he wasn't a tolerant person. He used to use the f-word with abandon, and he thought gay sex was unnatural. (Apparently, he never read about the gay penguins at the zoo.) It came as a surprise to me during our drives when my dad mentioned his "gay doctor friend." He did make sure to add "I don't like that he gossips too much," which was ironic coming from him, because half our conversations involved him telling me about which neighbors were cheating on their partners. However, this simple acknowledgement gave me hope maybe he was more progressive and tolerant than I thought. Maybe I'd come out to him, and before we'd know it, we'd be watching episodes of *RuPaul's Drag Race* together.

During his final week of chemo, my dad said, "I have to talk to you about something serious."

I hoped this could be my opening. "What's up?"

"In case things take a turn for the worse, I don't want to end up on life support."

I was nonplussed.

"Dad, it's not going to get that bad. The doctor said things are looking good."

"I'm serious. I've worked in a hospital, and I've seen people on life support who are basically vegetables. If I get to that point, I don't want to live like that."

"Okay, I promise. "

At the end of the five weeks, the doctor said my dad needed time to rest so his body could heal. I still made sure to set aside a couple days a week either to see him in person or talk to him on the phone. I noticed his weight loss, his decreased appetite, his lack of energy. I worried, but surely it was just part of the healing process. Of course, he'd get better, we'd have our breakthrough coming out talk and embrace like sitcom characters.

When my dad called in late August, I thought he was just confirming our drive.

"I'm not feeling well. I have to go to the hospital."

I took him to the emergency room and watched a team of doctors poke and prod at him. He looked slight and sallow. His hair, always perfectly barbered, was a mess. His eyes seemed vacant.

We arrived at the hospital on Wednesday, but I had booked a weekend of shows starting Friday. Now I had doubts about leaving.

"I can cancel the shows if you need me to."

"Why cancel the shows? I'll probably be out of here in a day. Don't worry about me," he said with a wheeze.

And sure enough, he was up and about on Thursday, annoying the nurses when they had to draw blood and administer shots.

"They're bad with needles, and the food is terrible!" he complained.

"I can still drop the shows, if you need me to."

"This is what you want to do! Go do your shows. I'll see you when you get back."

On Friday, I traveled to Massachusetts and had one of the best sets I'd had in ages. It was a relief to feel normal for a moment, at home with a microphone in my hand. After the show, I got a call from my mom.

"Your dad slipped into a coma. Can you come home tonight?"

Without a second thought, I jumped on an overnight bus and arrived early Saturday morning. By then, my dad was awake, if not fully aware of his surroundings. He continued to insist.

"I'll be okay."

I could tell it was different this time, though. Attached to his arm was an IV drip connected to a large red package.

"I had to have a blood transfusion. I don't feel clean about it."

The staff suggested my mother and I go home for the time being. I didn't realize until I looked in a mirror that I looked bedraggled and exhausted, wearing a wrinkled sweater with crust still on my eyes. I got home and immediately passed out. I spent the night cycling through dreams like a channel flipper until I woke up at 1 a.m. with a start. I instinctively reached for my phone, which rang as soon as I held it. It was the hospital.

"Are you able to come in right now? We have some news about your dad."

The tone was neutral, but the message was pretty clear.

I meet my mother at the hospital and waited for what felt like an eternity for the doctor to arrive. She told us my dad slipped into another coma and had an internal hemorrhage.

"We are doing everything we can, but we want you to be prepared in case things take a turn for the worse."

We sat at his bedside, still as gargoyles. Several hours later, a different doctor called us into the hallway. She had braids and a slight Caribbean accent.

Somehow, it felt fitting to see his life in her hands.

"Unfortunately, your father isn't responding well to the blood transfusion or any of the other treatments we are giving him. I know this is difficult, but we need to discuss the options of either putting him on life support or choosing not to resuscitate," she said.

And there was that word again. *Options.* Except I knew, at that point, this was not an option; this was a formality. Tears filling her eyes, my mother looked at me, waiting for me to make the call. I remembered what my father told me earlier and made the decision that breaks my heart to this day.

We sat in the room in silence, waiting for the EKG to stop beeping.

I spoke to my dad one last time, at his wake. I expected it to be relatively small, but I was shocked by how many of his co-workers came out. I gave a brief eulogy and invited anyone who wanted to speak to come to the stage. Immediately, the room filled with stories about my father. One nurse told a story about how my dad tackled a drug addict who attacked her. My dad's friend talked about a road trip they took that reminded me of the trips I had with him those last few weeks.

My mother closed with a funny anecdote about how they met in high school. My dad followed her around for weeks, begging to go on a date with her. I imagined their 30-plus-year relationship, from their first apartment to having me to changing careers and buying a house. My mother left the lectern, and I was jarred from my reverie.

I trudged back up to the podium like a morbid emcee, thanked everyone for their kind words, and announced there would be a repast around the corner.

Once everyone left the room, I knelt at the casket. Without an audience, I was finally able to find the words. I leaned in close and whispered into his ear, "I love you, and I'll miss you ... and, oh, by the way, I'm gay."

I stood there, clutching the side of the pine box, just wanting to hear his reaction or one of his wise-ass remarks, but knowing it was not going to come.

And never before have I wished harder for any other option.

TROUBLE BLONDE

by Jeena Bloom

I'm driving up the hill on the 405, ready to make my way into the San Fernando Valley. I tap my fingers on the steering wheel along to the beat of a song that was cool 10 years ago. A Toyota Camry with a gnarly rear fender rockets diagonally across four lanes of traffic to make an exit. Red tail lights pop on and off like Christmas lights. The roof of my Hyundai scrapes the black cloud of soot that hangs just over the top of the freeway.

I descend.

I know the Valley about as well as I know any other place on Earth. You descend the hill from regular Los Angeles and enter the Valley's crosscutting miles of strip malls and high-mileage strip clubs. It is a singular, unsexy place, despite its porny reputation. Asphalt, baked white in the sun and hot to the touch, connects you from one El Pollo Loco to the next. Even the street names of the deep Valley lack the louche romanticism of the boulevards of LA proper. No glamour is to be found on Sherman Way, no celebrities to be spotted on Vanowen and Saticoy Streets.

It is, for the second time in my life, home.

I freshen up and change. I drive the 20 minutes from my apartment in Van Nuys to a barrel-shaped restaurant in Burbank to meet a guy for drinks. He's paunchy and wears a flannel shirt, even though its over 90 that day. He gives me an awkward hug, his body leaning far forward with his legs planted firm and far away from me. He has a look on his face I immediately recognize: he's already decided he's getting laid tonight.

We talk, drink craft beers, and tell our stories. He lets it drop, quite unsubtly, that he's a friend of the actor Randall Park. I'm slightly impressed, but then he immediately corrects himself: he's actually a friend of a friend of Randall Park. We fuck anyway. What else are you going to do with yourself when you're a pretty lady, aging rapidly, and unemployed in the San Fernando Valley?

I left Los Angeles eight years ago as a sad, confused man. I came back, eight years later, as a much happier (but still frequently confused) transgender woman. I'm not a natural blonde, but I had been flirting with the color for almost two years before returning to Los Angeles. Within a week of moving back, I went as blonde as I could go without breaking my hair. I looked in the mirror and blew myself a kiss. I was finally living the life of a Trouble Blonde.

Before my date with the friend of the friend of Randall Park, I was in the west LA beach adjacent community of Playa Vista. I have a weird history with this neighborhood. It was a brand new development when I saw it last, a haven for rich kids with loft apartments they could never afford on their own talent. In the eight years since my last visit, it had become the hub of the Los Angeles tech industry. I was there for a full day of interviews with a tech company.

Not just any company, but one that once fired me as a man, now wanting to talk to me about working for them as a woman.

I came to Los Angeles with four months of severance from my old company in Manhattan. I managed to take that four months of salary and made it last nearly three. I was desperate for work and money, but even still, I applied to this company more as a joke. But the recruiter called me in anyway. The company name and my time working there appeared on my resume, but based on our conversations to that point, I have to assume they thought I was a brand new person.

As a trans lady, my voice is naturally rather deep for a woman, but after a year of speech therapy, I talk in a slightly-affected deep vocal fry, like if Kathleen Turner stayed up for three nights straight. It's a tech company, so I went all in: black turtleneck, blonde hair, intense eyes. I was doing the full Elizabeth Holmes, and I decided I was going to hypnotize these guys into accidentally giving me my job back.

I interviewed with the boss of the department. Let's call him RJ. He's skyscraper tall, brush cut that adds another two inches of height. RJ's a pure geek. (He told me about a 1/4th scale working R2D2 that his robot club built together.) He read my resume. He asked me tech questions. I gave him solid answers. I looked him in the eye, joked confidently. I searched his eyes for recognition of the former me. Nothing.

I used to hang out by his cubicle and make fun of the bosses with him. I'm pretty sure we smoked weed together in the parking lot. He told me stories about cases I worked on, about people he didn't know I knew. He didn't know who I was.

Finally, he asked me about my previous company experience. He asked me which boss I used to work for. I gave him the name of my ex-boss. Let's call him Vikram. I prayed Vikram left when the company was bought out by its new corporate parent. "Oh, cool," RJ said, "He still works here. I'm sure he'll be excited to see you again." My heart sank. Vikram fired me and will remember.

I also met another engineer working under RJ. He grilled me on my tech skills. I passed. He told me he used to work for Vikram, too; he had started around the time I was working remotely and was about to be fired. He asked, "Were you around when James was here?" His voice betrayed a tinge of contempt. This was an infamous name, it seemed, in the history of Vikram's ex-employees. It also used to be my name.

He was talking about me.

Tech interviews are brutal affairs. They sit you down for wave after wave of bosses and adjacent employees grilling you about separate parts of the job and the company. I once interviewed with Google for two full days in a row for a job I didn't get. The interviews with RJ were nice, though; it was like talking with an old friend. It actually *was* talking with an old friend, but I was the only one who felt that way. RJ told me if he could, he would hire me on the spot. Score one for Elizabeth Holmes, the tech industry's most noteworthy Trouble Blonde.

But I had to wait for the final word, and I knew the ruse wouldn't hold up. They'd ask Vikram about me, they would check my social security number, they would figure me out. I resigned myself to not getting the job, but regardless of the outcome, it was going to be a long wait. So, I fired up my dating and hookup apps and scheduled some distractions.

The friend of a friend of Randall Park didn't really do it for me, so instead I decided to give a shot to a guy I dubbed Chris Rocks in my contacts on my phone. Chris Rocks looked like a stereotypical '80s hair rocker and nothing like the comedian Chris Rock. I gave him that name myself. Chris

Rocks was also a real rocker; he played in some local band that apparently tore it up in the Encino metro area. Chris Rocks would be my distraction while I waited for word back from this job, and I'd be ruining his life just like Trouble Blondes had been doing to musicians since the invention of peroxide.

I was ready to, in a word, rock.

Chris Rocks apparently was not. As it turns out, Chris Rocks rock band played almost exclusively covers of TV theme songs and Weird Al parodies. My hot rocker dude was actually an enormous dork. And not a dork in the way hot girls say their boyfriends are "total dorks" because they once watched *Iron Man 3* on an airplane and are really good at cunnilingus. Chris Rocks was the genuine article. I wanted a rock star to make each other miserable for two weeks with tequila and hiking trail sex; what I got instead was a two-week tour of the comic book stores of the San Fernando Valley and dinner at a sushi restaurant that was also somehow part of an Autozone. (We did do hand stuff on a hiking trail one time.)

Somehow my brief career as a dangerous LA vixen was coming up short due to my ability to attract only the most hopeless of hopeless dweebs. The irony was not lost on me.

Flashback: the seventh grade. I was the most hopeless of the hopeless dweebs in the entire school. At that age, I would find growing up to be a thirtysomething adult that plays Weird Al covers in a garage band in Encino, CA to be the height of unattainable cool. Young me would wish to grow up to have game that tight. I was a scrawny little dude, pre-transition, taped glasses, and an encyclopedic knowledge of all of the monsters found in the bestiary canon of *Dungeons and Dragons.*

Mindy was the first Trouble Blonde I had ever met. She was in three of my classes in seventh grade. She was frequently seen making out with ninth graders — *a full two grades ahead of her.* She could be withering and bitchy in the way seventh-grade girls can be and cut the boys to their cores. The boys were scared of her, and they wanted her in equal measure. I was scared of her and wanted her too, but in my own special way. I didn't want her to be mine. I wanted her to be me. I wanted to replace her.

She never had much to say to me, except to demand answers on the algebra quizzes. I watched her destroy the egos of the seventh grade boys and devour the tongues of the ninth grade boys with equal parts envy and awe. We had gone an entire school year barely speaking until one Sunday afternoon, my mom sent me to the mall to pick up some new sneakers. She handed me some cash and dropped me off at the mall and left me to my own devices. After walking up and down that entire small town Indiana mall, I finally found a pair that met my internal sense of style: white high-tops with gold buttons and red and black snakeskin patterns on the toes and heel. Those shoes were as gay as Indiana would legally allow at the time, and I purchased them right away. I even chipped in part of my own allowance since they were a little over budget.

Satisfied in my fabulous fashion sense, I treated myself to the McDonalds in the mall. I had my tray and my bag of shoes swinging from my wrist and was looking for a place to sit when I heard a familiar voice say "Hey, kid."

It was Mindy, of course, and she damn well knew my name, having stolen the answers off my quizzes for months. I turned and stammered out something that sounded like

"Hey, what's up?" and she pointed to the chair next to her, silently ordering me to sit next to her and keep her company.

I don't remember exactly what we talked about at first, but eventually she asked to see my very homosexual shoes. Her eyes lit up, and she demanded that I let her borrow them sometime. Then she pointed at some older boy working at the register I had been checking out earlier. She asked me if I thought he was cute, and I nearly choked on my Quarter Pounder. In that second, I dreamed we'd become best friends, and she'd tell me all the secrets of her gender.

After that day, I never spoke to her again.

I'd befriend and even try to date Trouble Blondes for years after that, with mostly middling success. I was too much of a closet case, too much of a DnD playing dork to really let myself free in their presence. It wasn't until I lived in LA eight years ago that any of that changed. I managed to work myself into a nice, full-blown case of sex addiction, hooking up with men in the finest LA parking garages. I was working as a computer nerd by day and filling my gross masculine body with Carl's Jr burgers by night. But, by late night, it was dessert with Brian in his apartment garage. I was finally coming out of my shell when I met her, the queen of Trouble Blondes.

Let's call her Joy. She was petite, barely 5'3". Joy was a professional graphic designer and semi-professional groupie for terrible, washed-up rock bands of the nineties. We met online and bonded over our love of gender variance and devouring men in parked cars. She lived in Las Vegas, just a few hours away from Los Angeles. After six months of foreplay, we decided to meet. She was staying in the brand new community of Playa Vista, the same fancy neighborhood where eight years later, I would interview in secret for my old job in Elizabeth Holmes drag. She was visiting a friend, a pudgy male friend who not-so-secretly wanted her for himself. He looked like the type to know his way around some Weird Al covers. Let's call him Danny.

Joy and I met for drinks at Danny's condo in Playa Vista, paid for entirely by his parents. The place was elegant, but I immediately noticed something really, really strange about Danny's place: he had all the doors removed. There were no doors on the bedrooms, no doors on the bathrooms, no doors on the closet. Just a front door. It would be enough to make a rational person run for their life, but Joy was giving me an undeniable energy: I was finally going to have sex with a Trouble Blonde. Now, if I could just find a way to switch bodies with her, I'd be crossing out my entire bucket list.

Danny retired for the evening to his doorless master bedroom, and Joy and I continued to vibe. We quickly retired to the doorless guest bathroom and got down to business. Clothes quickly came off. Tongues met. Bodies pressed together. Joy's phone vibrated to life. I was halfway inside her when she looked at her phone and said with barely a hint of emotion: "Danny's texting me. He can hear us having sex. He's crying."

"Should we stop?" I ask her.

She doesn't even bother to respond. She just pulls me back down onto her and we kept going at it. Too bad about that no doors thing, though.

Danny glowered in the doorway watching us. Then he grabbed me by the neck and threw me out into the hall of his building naked. A few seconds later, my clothes followed.

At breakfast the following morning, I told one of my buddies about the night before. He was in awe. He'd always thought I was a dud with the ladies and was amazed that I had managed to get through this entire night without running away screaming back to Burbank. I told him that my Trouble Blonde days were over. It was fun, but too stressful. I told my friend I was retiring from my life of danger and going back to the quiet life of an inveterate dork.

Joy set up our next date about two hours later.

We'd be together for five years.

She ruined my life.

I'd never go so far as to blame Joy for getting me fired, but the chaos of our relationship created the environment that made me so bad at my job that it led to my firing. We floated another three years after my job in LA let me go, living at her parents' place in Georgia and then in our own place in Tennessee. I lived as a male that entire time, trying to be the good suburban husband to my reformed Trouble Blonde wife. We put up a fairly decent front: a condo, a Lexus, a prominent place as the cool couple in our small church. Things couldn't last, and we finally split up. It was six months later that I moved to New York City, and a month after that I began my gender transition.

Five years later, I was back in LA, living out my own Trouble Blonde life with a series of men that were remarkably (and disappointingly) similar to the guy I used to be. I lacked Joy's confidence and magnetism to properly ruin any of these men's lives, even the 50-year-old guy who was way too into Billie Eilish. If there was ever anybody who was up for a life ruining, it was a middle-aged, straight, male Billie Eilish fan.

The longer it took for them to respond, the more I really wanted my job back. I didn't just need the money (although I desperately needed money), but I needed the job. I lived in LA in the closet the last time and never got to do it right.

I wanted that second chance, but I knew that they would eventually talk to Vikram. They would figure me out.

I passed the time waiting for them to call. I booked some standup shows. I hooked up with a male comic with TV credits. I didn't think he wanted to be seen in public with me.

The recruiter called a week later. She had news: RJ was impressed. The other engineer was impressed. Everybody was impressed. But then she paused and her tone darkened. "We talked to Vikram," she said. "And we have some questions."

They wanted to know what happened. I couldn't tell them that I had been spending my whole life chasing the type of woman I wanted to become. I couldn't tell them that once I found my own Trouble Blonde, the chaos of that relationship was too much for me to handle and caused them to fire me. I couldn't tell them that in the long wait for them to give me an answer, I learned that blonde hair or not, I was just not the troublesome type and had somehow become a dork magnet in Los Angeles. So I told them some version of the truth. I had been living a lie. The stress was too hard for me. It was all the closet's fault. They said they would get back to me in a week.

I spent that entire week sexually pleasing the most socially-awkward men of the San Fernando Valley, with not one ruined life among them.

Anyway, I got the job.

RJ stuck his neck out for me, and I got my second chance. I can be the person I was always meant to be, and I can do it in the city I love most. I'm a woman working for a company that once fired me when I was a man. They even gave me an 85% raise versus what I used to make when I worked there before. As a woman, I'm worth nearly twice as much to them as when they knew me as a man. I think I accidentally fixed feminism.

I work in Playa Vista, the neighborhood where I finally fell in love with a Trouble Blonde, and commute home to Van Nuys. I dyed my hair back to black and stopped ineptly trying to ruin lives. My taste in men has not improved.

I reach the top of the hill. The roof scrapes that black cloud, and I descend. I pound the steering wheel to the beat of a song that was never, not once, cool. I'm on my way home. If you see me around, and you don't recognize in my face the other person I used to be, don't worry.

This is the only me there is now.

WATER DAMAGE

by David Perez

A few months ago, I was at the bar where I pick up my vegetable share, and a man struck up a conversation. I came for the organic veggies and stayed for a gin gimlet or two (four), when this handsome corn-fed stranger noticed the lock screen image on my phone.

"Is that your dog?" he smiled. The picture was a dog I named Mikey, a border collie wearing a birthday hat licking a small birthday cake with yogurt frosting made to look like carrots.

"She used to be my dog," I said into gimlet 2.5.

There is a part of me that has stopped protecting strangers from the weight of my experiences. "My brother? Dead!" "My sister … also dead!" If I calculated the minutes spent stuffing my truths down in my gut to make sure someone is not inconvenienced by my grief, I could fill a year.

I have stopped doing that.

"She used to be my dog. She died. Recently. And it was the worst day of my life."

He still looked hot when his face was rattled.

"Ohhh, I am so sorry," his eyes sharpened and stared down at the bar seeming to say *fuck*. I looked at his mouth and wondered … *how straight is he really, and can I suck his dick?*

"I am so sorry," he said crestfallen.

I didn't keep my grief to myself.

I have a lot of grief, and sometimes I don't know where to put it. I grieve for my two siblings who both, a decade apart, lost their lives to addiction. I grieve for my step-father who died in a plane crash. I grieve for Mikey.

I work from home, so my days are simultaneously endless and short. I rarely wear pants, and if it wasn't for my boyfriend Steve I would go feral and never shower. I am a comedian, which goes first in this sentence even though the way I make my money is that I own a business where I help people get jobs in advertising. I have two identities running alongside each other, colliding and competing for my anxiety.

The working from home problem: *getting out of bed.* Not in the "stare at the ceiling with existential dread" variety (that comes later, stay tuned, watch this space), but the "staying in bed that happens when you are accountable to no one but yourself" variety. I have complained about being over-worked on days that I have watched several hours of porn that featured affable straight guys having anal experiences for what I assume to be forty-seven dollars. I have also worked for 17 hours straight and forgotten to brush my teeth for three days. Structure is an issue.

In the height of this lack of balance, I thought I needed to force some sort of structure and routine into my life. "Should I get a dog?" I said to a college friend whose Boston terrier regularly tried to sexually assault my mouth. One Sunday, I went to the Union Square Petco on purpose because that friend sent me a picture of a dog she saw at a previous adoption event. I went and immediately saw her goofy face, pink freckle on her nose, and large dumb tongue, and I knew that this dog would be mine. The tether was instant. So fast. Faster than most relationships. I looked into her eyes and knew that I would be her person and spend the rest of her life picking up her feces first thing in the morning.

Too fast.

I loved this dog, and, as you know, this dog dies. Does telling your good stories prevent you from feeling the ache of the bad ones? Does talking about your love keep it alive, or does it make it threadbare? I would like to retain that love even if it means I never get over the pain.

Too fast.

I went to Union Square Petco, I got the dog, I named her Mikey after my friend who left NYC (a sequel to a tradition — my friend named her cat Dave when I left Seattle). I brought her home, and she was a delightful nightmare. Steve and I instantly created 10-12 nicknames for her — confusing for a dog trying to learn her own name: Mikey, Michael, Mikey Skittles, Baby, My Baby, Morky, Princess, Mocosa, the list is endless. She became the center of my schedule and a financial burden that I adored. She shat on the floor. She ate a dead baby pigeon off the street, she startled and knocked over a toddler, she grabbed a pizza out of a stranger's hand, she ate a tennis ball and pooped a mosaic of bright green spots for one whole week. She filled her crate with diarrhea, she filled her crate with vomit, she filled my day with work. She begged at the fridge three times a day for her favorite treat: a single piece of ice. Mikey put the cube in her mouth, let it melt for a second and then dropped it on the floor, letting a puddle emerge; then she devoured it.

Every morning, hangover or not, she pawed at my sleeping face at 7:27 a.m. on the dot, bullying me into emptying a can of duck and sweet potato slop into a bowl for her to inhale. I opened the door to our apartment, and she bolted down the stairs. Out we would go to the dog park where she dug and played, and I enjoyed empty conversation with people I would normally never interact with. She ran in ferocious circles while I listened to the women of Greenpoint (all dressed like Dr. Quinn Medicine Woman) talk about how their dog Byron is doing "great on leash." I enjoyed this, though. Spending the first moments of my day in McGolrick Park seemed like an anchor. I had a shared spot on the bench, though it was unspoken, reserved for me and the three other people whose company I actually enjoyed. Our bond was created over talking shit about the woman in tie dye leggings who never picked up her dog's turds. I'd have an Americano and watch the trees of McGolrick change. Two years. Get up, walk the baby, get home, give her ice, start my day.

The routine was an orbit I enjoyed.

Too much.

You have to understand something about me. I am equally affable and unknowable, and this is not me being mysterious or cool, God knows I am neither of those things. (I do improvisational comedy, the cost of which is *never being cool*). I am capable of meeting a stranger, performing whomever they need me to be for no more than 34 days, growing tired of it, then shifting back into a curated/guarded state. Like a sociopath without the blood lust.

Like most fat, gay children who turned into fat, gay adults, there is a lacquer of protection that surrounds me, and that lacquer can be funny, irreverent David who likes the dark side of a joke, or it can be cold and uninterested and maybe even mean David. Both are designed to minimize the impact of not being important to another person. I have great friends in my life who I assume have silently accepted that proximity to me is on a rotation — open, then closed, open again, closed again. It is like boarding a train: sometimes you just have to wait for an empty car.

I have built an identity around protecting myself from love because I never thought it was in the cards for me. I have spent an eternity (ages fifteen through thirty-five) trying to fuck and love dudes whom I thought I wanted to *be with* but ultimately I just wanted to *be*. What a fucking nightmare trying to cradle the crotch of someone who has lived inside the beauty bubble you never inhabited. Maybe if I could capture the love of someone adored by the world, I wouldn't be invisible? If I could retain the love of someone extraordinary, maybe I wouldn't be so forgettable? My lust for tall, skinny darlings and effortless, beautiful boys was a dodge, just me running from a fat shadow directly towards a void.

I told a friend one day, smugly "stop loathing who you aren't, and start loving who you are." Advice I could never take.

Before Steve, I pursued/fucked/longed for unavailable men, a short list that includes:

- *Straight men*
- *Men with boyfriends*
- *Men with debilitating addictions*
- *Co-workers*
- *Closeted Mormons*
- *Newly-gay Mormons*
- *A man who stapled a sleeping bag over his windows instead of buying curtains*

- *An ultimate frisbee player*
- *Two professional clowns*
- *A self-described witch that jerked me off with almond butter*

A murderers row of disappointment.

After getting dumped by a basic twink at a bar called Basik (a bit on the nose right?), I decided to take the psychic weight of love off my shoulders and resign myself to dying alone watching *Rizzoli & Isles* in a Barcalounger, a blanket over my legs, two cats eating my decomposing knuckles. I decided to embrace that fat shadow.

Two days before New Year's Eve, I downloaded this super sophisticated piece of technology called Tinder, and the first person I matched with was Steve, who had, by some weird coincidence, downloaded it the same night, his first match being me. Nine months later, he moved into my Greenpoint apartment, and I politely asked my roommate, a self-described mystic (which just means she knows where to buy incense) to move out. A month before he moved in, I went to Petco, and I met Mikey, and the puzzle of my happiness assembled before my eyes, and suddenly I wanted to be me for the first time. I took a picture of Mikey and Steve on the couch, and it stayed on my lock screen until her first birthday.

I am certain that dogs exist in the world to help people access the purest parts of their love. They have a direct path to our hearts, because their love is uncomplicated and unfettered. Yes, we feed them, protect them, pull various things from the hair around their buttholes, and people argue that your dog just loves you because you take care of them. I'm sure that logic is backed up by science, but I couldn't give less of a shit. My tether was something else. Mikey was my uncomplicated soulmate.

A month before Mikey's second birthday, my phone rattled at four in the morning, and my step-mom, groggy-voiced, eeked out "Lisa overdosed … and she is on life support. You got to come home." I would like to pretend that I didn't expect that to happen, but that would just be one huge fucking lie.

Thirty-five hours later, I was in a tiny Orange County hospital that smelled like Salisbury steak, saying goodbye to my sister. I held her hand and played "Time After Time" on my phone and told her I love her. At 10 p.m. on the dot, she stopped breathing, and my idiot father made a joke that she "made curfew." I did not cry the entire time. I hugged my nephews, my mom, my dad, my everyone, while they wept, but I didn't cry. Not once. I got on a plane and got home, opened the door and Mikey ran down the hall and jumped into my lap and whined and cried, because she missed me just a bit less than I missed her, and I cried for what seemed to be two to three days. Steve, Mikey, and I huddled in bed, and I thanked whatever ephemeral God there is that my tiny family was intact.

Too much.

"Can I ask how she died," the corn-fed stranger asked as I waved down the bartender for gimlet number three. "I mean, you can. But if you do, I am gonna tell you the truth, and it's fucked up."

He stared into a beer he had described as an "approachable IPA," which makes my dick so flaccid it retreats into my body.

"OK, I can handle it."

I want you to know that how I feel about how she died is unreasonable and equally impossible for me to navigate. Plainly put: I think her death is my fault, and no amount of reassurance from Steve or my friends or anyone who reads this can convince me otherwise. Even the therapist who I fired for lotioning her legs during our sessions for the second time couldn't convince me.

Too slow.

One unremarkable morning, Mikey put her paw on my face. I begrudgingly got up. I poured her slop into a bowl. I winced at the noise of the contractors below, renovating the apartment. I hated those guys, because they left the front door open, tracked dust on the stairs and screamed at each other in Mandarin while I tried to work. Mikey went to the door, and I got her leash and my keys and went back for my hat. I opened the door, and, as routine, she ran down the stairs, her nails rattling and clacking on the worn linoleum. But when I got downstairs, I realized the door had been left open, and I saw her awkward little hips round the corner of the door and gallop toward the park, which was across McGuinness Avenue, a four lane intersection. And a truck route.

Too fast.

You know she is dead, and I assume you can put together how. The details of which I have a hard time forgetting, and they visit me in my dreams despite how many gimlets I drink to keep them away. The vet, who was by luck a block from where she was hit, said she didn't experience pain because shock had set in. I also paid $500 on the spot to make sure she had fentanyl, because she was mine. Steve arrived 30 minutes later, and for 12 minutes we thought she was gonna make it.

She didn't.

Her pink tongue turned grey, an image I would empty my savings account to erase. They offered to cremate her in one big batch "with cats, hamsters, and other dogs," and I immediately put $900 on my credit card to have her cremated alone. We went home, I took off my clothes, covered with the gore of the day, and put them in a garbage bag. We went to see a movie at a place where we could order never-ending drinks to our seats, and we cried in the dark, leaving the movie early to walk around the neighborhood that no longer felt like ours. We avoided the apartment that suddenly wasn't home.

Eight days later, we picked her up, now in a plastic bag inside of a purple tin can.

I stayed in bed. I stared at the ceiling. I never went back to the park. I saw some of the people I know from the park and ignored them on the street. I forced myself to walk across that intersection and felt empty after 15 steps. I watched two seasons of *The Great British Baking Show* in one sitting. We put everything that resembled Mikey into a box and kept it out of reach of accidental discovery. Suddenly the apartment was an empty monument to another era. It was dust, it was debris, it was light leaving across the ceiling.

We moved apartments, and, after cleaning the old place, Steve and I stood in the threshold of the unlit living room where our little family lived. I held him from behind, and we cried while the saws of the contractors, working late, rattled under our feet.

Too much.

"That is really fucked up" the corn-fed guy said looking at his phone.

We shared a silence.

He looked at the door to the adjacent room, bad music trailing out every time the door opened.

"Do you know what band is playing in there tonight?"

Undoubtedly, he was wishing he was in there and not directly inside of my bullshit. I understood. I would want out of that conversation, too.

I went home to our new apartment, put the veggies in their place and made myself a drink. I walked into my still unpacked living room, and Mikey's ashes sat dull on the top of the bar. We were having a New Year's Party, and having her ashes there seemed grim for embarking on the new year. I took the can and put it on the top shelf of book shelves I installed in my office, poorly. I turned to leave the room, looked back at the shelves, and all six of them collapsed in slow motion, a mess that pulled plaster from the walls, scattered every book, shattered glasses and sent the can of what used to be Mikey across the floor. Remarkably the can didn't open, just dented. One last slap in the face from this terrible year.

Too bad.

I am mad in a way that I can't really make contact with. I find myself filled with rage and then cold, numb departure. There is really the smallest of openings where I let people get close, and those openings relocate and close up and vanish. Mikey was the way in. Mikey was the prism I reflected my light off for other people to see. That space, I mourn and I miss.

Putting yourself back in orbit seems impossible, but also inevitable. I am trying to take the advice I have given: "You're allowed to take a shit, but you can't roll around in it." It's been almost a year, and I anticipate the anniversary date like someone has scheduled a sob into my calendar.

We will scatter her ashes at the beach or keep them forever. There isn't a space between. Those decisions linger.

I am out of bed. It's easier now, because my dreams are frequently nightmares, where I am wandering somewhere, with a phone that doesn't work trying to find Steve who has left for good. The things I love go away, that's what my brain says, though my brain is an unreliable narrator.

I am out of bed and into the world and telling jokes about the worst day of my life. I send a clip of my stand up set to a friend, and I tell this joke:

"I lost 47 lbs this year!!! (audience applauds) That's how much my dog weighed."

(Silence)

My friend: "I think it's too soon for you." And I can tell that she is right but I'm telling jokes because I can't roll around in the shit. I won't.

We get a new dog, who we name Tina. She is tiny and looks like a little bear, with ragged little ears and dreadlocks near her butthole. I am learning to love her. She hates the park, and shits in two spots, one of them being our living room. We eventually take the toys of Mikey we couldn't throw away and couldn't see and lay them on Tina's bed. She holds them in her mouth, but doesn't destroy them. She surrounds herself with them like she is having a seance. One night I have three to seven vodkas and tell Tina about her sister. I instantly feel pathetic and also lost as fuck.

Mikey is gone, and that is something I can't negotiate. She is stuck in the ether of my love, floating above me like a risk I took and a bet I lost. In this next era, when I make a drink and an ice cube falls to the floor, she isn't there to eat it; it just slides under the fridge to melt somewhere slowly. A puddle, then a drop, then just water damage.

A few weeks ago, I went to pick up my vegetables, and I ordered a gimlet and the corn-fed stranger was there. He was nice, but it's clear a conversation was out of the question, as if my darkness was contagious. I grabbed my gimlet, and swallowed it in one obnoxious drink.

"Look, I changed my lock screen," I shouted, almost shoving it in his face. The picture is now of Steve and Tina, four eyes staring back at me, telling me it's OK to stay in bed.

"We got a new dog."

I put my gimlet down. The ice crashed and swiveled making a slow fading rattle.

I went home to see my little family.

FREE O/B/O: GREAT, SIMPLE, SOLID WOODEN BOOKSHELF; HAS SEEN SOME GAY SEX; *MIGHT* BE HAUNTED (ASTORIA, NY)

by Timothy Dunn

Ok, hellooooo, Craigslist! Let's sell sell sell, right? Haha! Ok! Here we go!

This beauty for sale here is a four-level bookshelf/ hutch-type situation. There is a back, the bottom opening is open and there are some old nails sticking out underneath, where an old piece of wood used to be, but just don't touch those parts, ok? It's a piece of furniture, people! Woo hoo! Whooptie-freaking-doo!

Her dimensions are 36" high x 32" long x 10.5" deep. There are four evenly-spaced shelves, and you can do that math.

I honestly don't know what kind of wood it is, but she's definitely solid and is sporting a nice grey/beige paint situation that I picked out *custom* to match a stripe in the brand new Pottery Barn linen duvet that I bought when I first moved to NYC in 2004! OMG, HAAAY! And, hey, I've had her for a long time, so she's sturdy … but she's gotten *lovingly* dinged up over the years! Like we all do in long-term relationships, amiright, gals? LOL but, no, she is GREAT, and she's yours for the low, low price of *FREE O/B/O*.

LOL I probs shouldn't tell *you* this, Craigslist Bargain Hunter, but now that I mentioned it, it's a little fucked up, actually, that I'd sell a piece of furniture that's been around me for so much of my growing up. I've had this little lady since...

Jesus Christ. Since...

...well, definitely since Chicago. Did I get her in ... 2003!?!?? Oh my GOD. Right out of college! Oh, what a trip! In 2003, I was a working as an actor in the Chicago theatre scene to pay the rent in that gorgeous loft apartment (with that BALCONY!) and the exposed ducts that I definitely couldn't afford, ordering "5 for $5" large pizzas from Little Caesars bc there wasn't much left after rent, hanging out with neighborhood trash bc I thought it was fun and dangerous and edgy and the opposite of my suburban, nouveau riche, Republican upbringing.

But, really, I was just getting drunk and being 22 and floundering, while I desperately tried to figure out how to live on my own in the real world. Desperately trying to figure out how to be "Out and Proud," and failing miserably. Desperately and fearfully trying to "just be safe," which was code for "just don't get AIDS," which seemed to top a lot of people's List of Concerns when I came out to them. And, maybe, also, I spent a good portion of those years still trying to figure out how *not* to be gay? It all just seemed like too much for one person to handle back then. It seemed like too daunting of a prospect, the thought that I'd somehow eventually find a way to be happy and successful and secure and accepted ... while also being gay? Like ... how?

Well, in 2003, a big part of the "how" for me was the the-atre. I truly, really owe my life to the friends that I made in the Chicago theatre scene in those years. I was some pretentious, hot-shot Northwestern University Theatre School graduate who thought he was Very Talented and Good, and they were ... actual artists. Actual professionals. And those artists became parents-by-proxy to a wounded little chorus boy who was entering Gay Puberty all by himself at 22 years old. They could've just turned their noses up at me and become Work Acquaintances, but they took me in. They invited me to eat lunch with them. They asked if I wanted to carpool. They'd put in duets with me when we'd crash karaoke bars. I'd never had that before. And, especially the fags, they didn't know they were doing it, but they were spoon-feeding me a much-needed dose of Gay Hope in those days. Showing me successful gay relationships. Successful gay careers. Showing me people who were gay who were not only "ok with it," but who were adamant about loving and embracing their gay-ness. These are the people who took a hot knife to the thick, heavy storm clouds that had been gathered around my head for years, and they sliced a tiny hole right through them for me, offering me a tiny sliver, a glimpse of the bright, blue sky that they were all somehow able to live underneath. Their happiness gave me something to work towards; their ease and their comfort inside their strange, gay skins gave me something to aspire to. And while I often felt like my brain was growing too fast, that too much was happening too quickly for me in those years, I distinctly remember being laser-focused on one thing: I could never let my parents see me floundering. And don't get me wrong — my parents are truly incredible. Supportive, loving, and even if they weren't particularly thrilled or terribly interested in knowing the details or hearing the specifics about My Homosexuality, if they somehow see this ad, I will be absolutely MORTIFIED, bc number one, my parents being on Craigslist is a bizarre and strange thought to me, but, number two, my parents would literally give me everything they have without a moment's hesitation, if I asked for it.

But I didn't want a gorgeous house in the suburbs. I didn't want a Big Fancy Job at a Fortune 500 company. I didn't want a Jeep Grand Cherokee. I didn't want what they had. (And, truthfully, I probably couldn't have had those things even if I'd wanted them, anyway, bc those things weren't ever *for* me.)

But I especially didn't want their help back then. Not just because I was stubborn and proud (I was), but because the help they were offering wasn't the help I needed. I didn't know what I needed, and, sure, maybe if I would have vocalized those struggles sooner, maybe they *could've* actually helped. But I didn't do that. I didn't want that.

What I *wanted* to do was to buy a scrubby little bookshelf at a second-hand furniture store somewhere on the north-west side of Chicago, and I wanted to paint it myself, and I wanted to figure out how to be a happy, gay-person, artist-type who found his way and made it "on" "his" "own." The drama of it all, bitches!

And, actually, now that I'm thinking about it, you guys … no, I had this bookshelf well before I had that apartment with the balcony. And, you guys? How about another round of sound for that gorgeous apartment with that gorgeous fucking balcony! Ugh! It was beautiful. That was my first and only balcony in my entire life. Man, I love Chicago so much. I miss it. I wish I had been older when I lived there. I wasn't ready for that kind of life yet. I had so much "figuring shit out" to do. I was barely keeping my head above water. I probably wasn't even doing a good job at that. I definitely wasn't.

So, yeah, I must've bought her before then. So, that means I've had this bookshelf since...

...yep.

...yep, I think I got these shelves when I was still dating Martin.

Martin. My very first boyfriend. LOL! Jesus Christ. Martin! Martin was a real, fucking asshole. He was married to a woman when I first met him, and he somehow didn't think to mention that fact until two months into dating me. And I was too young and dumb to connect the dots that quickly. Very kewl! So, yeah, he was a piece of shit. A real, proper, Royal Turd of a man. But. He was my *first* Royal Turd, so I hadn't figured out how to handle those kinds of Royal Turds-slash-manipulators-slash-pathological-liars yet, so we stayed together for three years. Fuck Martin, man. Lol. I was 19, and he was 26 when we met. And he was interested in ME??? Like, I'm cool and funny and everything, but Eyeroll_Emoji.gif. What a fucking mess he was. Eh. I hope he's doing ok now, though, I guess. We were kids. And the last time I ever heard from him, he called to tell me that he had adopted a kid of his own. And! That he was naming her one of the names we'd picked out to name "our kids" way-back-when! Ugh. Can you imagine? What a freaking psycho! LOL

OMG! And then, years later, after he and I had broken up (well, I broke up with him when his cheating and lying got too flagrant and too embarrassing for me to live with, which was Very Fun And Cute For Me!), I bumped into him at a gay bar with some of his friends, and purely out of spite, I took his best friend home with me and we did sex stuff omg IN FRONT OF THIS BOOKSHELFFFFFF!!!!!! OH my fucking GODDDDD!!!!

So, I've def had this bookshelf since before the balcony apartment, then. So, that means I was in college, and I moved out of the dorms my junior year! So, 2001! YES! Oh, what was our fucking landlord's name in our college apartment? Barry Goldman? Something like that? Mr. G! Oh man! :) I had never had a landlord before, and he was *exactly* what I had expected. We were kids, but he treated us like adults, though, and I guess we appreciated someone actually being hard on us in those years. Yes! I had that stupid *loft bed* in that apartment (Huge_Embarassing_Groan.mp3), and I actually think I bought this bookshelf bc I needed a little shelf for that part where the top of the lofted bed meets the ceiling of the room? Oh my GOD! This bookshelf was my freaking *HEADBOARD* from 2001-2003, gals!!! HOW did I forget that until right now??? LOL So, this bookshelf was UP IN MY BED, peeping some of my very first instances at sexxxxx with menzzzzzzz! Like, this lady was on the front lines of My First Gay Sexings™!

Now, you don't know me, and I'm sure you probably assume I'm some rich and debonair bon vivant, living in some skyscraper in Paris now, with the wind somehow barely ruffling my perfectly coiffed hair as I type this onto a typewriter at a measly 26 years of age … and you are … correct. ;) No no no, I live in Queens now, and I'm still acting and writing (Can_You_Believe.gif), but let me assure you that 2001-2003 were truly some *wild* years for me, ok? That was the very beginning of everything for me. Everything was a first.

There was that "straight" guy that I spent the summer with, who told me that he loved me as we breathlessly clutched onto each other, desperately tangling ourselves together in my bed, basking in the glow of young, dumb, freshly-minted, collegiate man-love. I can still smell his cologne. And his chest hair. His was the first hairy chest that I had ever been naked with. He went back to his girlfriend at the end of the summer. His girlfriend was a friend of mine, and turns out? They'd never actually broken up. But I kinda knew that already; she found out about us. She was devastated. I very much regret doing that to her. (He called me a few years ago, out of the blue. He has kids and a wife now. Ok!)

And before that, there was Connor. Oh, man. :) I fell in love with Connor when I was a freshman in college, way before I ever met Martin or the hairy chested man. Man, I loved Connor, but Connor told me again and again that it could never work out between us. He was the President of the Young Republicans on campus, and he was going into the US Armed Forces and a career in politics after school. So, A Gay Life, with or without me, wouldn't ever be an option for him. Oh man, he really broke my heart. I remember laying on the beach in the middle of the night in the middle of winter with him. He was a senior, and I was a freshman, and he would only call me when he was drunk. And only from payphones. (No one had cellphones yet back then, you ungrateful little punks!) He'd call my dorm room landline, and I would drop what I was doing and run-- RUN!-- to him, wherever he was. Boozy and breathless, he'd trace my face with his fingertips, kiss my nose, "jokingly" call me "baby." We'd walk hand-in-hand, something I'd never done with a man, always careful to stay in the shadows, far away from streetlights or any undergrads who might recognize us (well, him). We'd stop to sit and cuddle and kiss on park benches when we were *sure* no one was around. He always tasted like gin and tonics, and we would spend hours just rubbing our faces together. Neither one of us had ever kissed someone with stubble before. I loved it. I loved him. Man, I loved him. And I told him so, late one night, when he was speech-slurringly drunk and we were laying on the beach on the shores of Lake Michigan. It was February in Chicago, the middle of winter, in the middle of the night, and there we were, laying side-by-side on the frozen sand. I'd never been in love with a man before. I still remember exactly the way I was positioned and the way my whole heart leaped out of my body when I told him. He kept on saying things like "we can't keep meeting," and "this can't happen," and "what's the point of this?" And I remember I rolled over onto my left side and looked at him and his big ears in the moonlight and said, "I think the point of this for me is that … I … I think I love you." He didn't even flinch. He kept looking straight up at the sky, and kinda half-belched, half-laughed, "Eh, no you don't. You're confused. You're too young to know what love even is, anyway. And we can't keep doing this." But he kept calling. And I kept running to him.

Every time I'd get back home from our midnight walks along Lake Michigan, I would lay in my bed and cry and swear to myself that I would never see him again. It hurt too much. It made no sense. I knew he loved me. I *knew* it! I FELT it. But … he couldn't let it be. And so, I moved on. I made myself move on. I hated it. I didn't know how to move on. But I told myself that it was What I Needed To Do. No one knew about Connor and me. No one knew about me at all, at that point. So, I couldn't talk to anyone about it. I didn't know what to do. But I had to do something. So, I made myself move on. I don't know.

And then I met Martin, and we dated for three years. Oof.

Connor came back from serving in the Middle East for a week's visit a few years later, right after Martin and I had broken up, and he and I finally consummated our previously-unrequited love in that little loft bed whilst these sweet little bookshelves looked on, but, by then, our once verdant field had gone to flower for me. Dating A Not Good Person for that long had really done a number on my brain and my heart. In our post-coital glow, Connor said the thing that I had dreamed about. He told me that he loved me. That he'd always loved me. He'd been so scared. But that he'd always considered me his boyfriend when he was abroad, even when he knew I was dating Martin. And now that I *wasn't* dating Martin anymore, he wanted to be my boyfriend officially. I told him I needed to think about it. The next morning, I said "no." And then we had the most heartbreaking brunch ever. Oof. (He's married now, too. To a man, don't worry. And he is really doing very well for himself. I can't really keep in touch with him anymore, but I'm so proud of him. He did it. He did the damn thing. I'm proud of Connor. I still love Connor. I'll always love Connor.)

And then, oooooh man, there was quiiiiiite a run. There was another closeted guy who made me swear on an actual Bible (lol) that I would never tell anyone about us, but who then told a bunch of people I was gay after I broke things off with him. There was the impossibly hot guy whose AOL screenname was AberCROTCHme who blocked me the morning after our first date, when I got too stoned and had sex with him on the couch in the basement of his mom's house while we "watched" that *Star Wars* movie with Jar-Jar Binks. (I've still never seen it.) There was Toddy, the very first guy I ever brought home from a gay bar. We met on Halloween at Roscoe's in downtown Chicago. He was dressed up as a Twister board (like, the game), and, in the morning, he told me I was too young for him to give his phone number to. (Ok!) Dave, my second boyfriend ever, was a pretty serious drunk, and he used to leave burritos and cheeseburgers on these hallowed bookshelves, "in case he got hungry in the middle of the night." But then he moved to Florida and thought it was ok to leave me waiting and stranded in the Ft. Lauderdale airport for three hours, and then he just up and stopped returning my phone calls all together when I finally got back home to Chicago. Bad job, Dave! (We've mended fences now, though. We text on the holidays.)

OMG! Also! Here's a Bonus LOL: Dave "secretly" smoked cigarettes, like a pack a day, but only in his house, and he always smelled SO MUCH like cigs. And! He would lie to my face whenever I'd ask him about it bc I could smell it and taste it on him! LOL What an idiot he must have thought I was. Have you ever slept next to a chain smoker who insisted that they didn't smoke? Lol Like, that STENCH, baby! That TASTE, honey! That actual SMOKE LINGERING IN THE AIR when I'd get to his apartment early, queen! But ... nope, no smokers here, ma'am! LOLLLLLL!!!!!!!!

Wait, actually? I'm actually really fucking this ad up! LOL! None of these stories are very good selling points! Maybe this thing is freakin' cursed! Haha!

No no no, I'm kidding! This bookshelf is fine! This bookshelf is great! I had so many great Firsts with Little Miss Shelf! I charged my very first cell phone on her shelves! Back when T9 was how we texted and when leaving your phone plugged in at home all day was how we did it. My stacks and stacks of plays and sheet music binders lived on these bookshelves! I framed my very first Equity contract after college and displayed it on the top shelf for a good, long time. I secretly nursed myself through the first weeks of mononucleosis in bed in front of these shelves, terrified and frantic because mono and HIV have the exact same symptoms, and then was relieved and exhausted when I got the actual results.

Hmmm.

Wait.

Ok.

Wait.

Um, sorry, everyone for doing this, you guys, but um. This ad might actually be called off now.

Bc is it INSANE for me to get rid of a piece of furniture that's been literally beside me for this many years??? And not just get rid of it! To SELL! IT! Like, make money off of her, my sister-in-shelf, My Herstorybookshelves???

Ok.

Oooooook, very Cool and Smooth, Tim. I mean, Jesus Christ. You were planning on selling a piece of your own history for *FREE O/B/O* fucking dollars? YUCK. So, that's the price of a lifetime of memories to you. You picked an actual number amount that you thought it was all worth? Gross. Tim, that's gross. Memories for sale! Pick-up only! Cash or Venmo! Ugh. Who are you becoming, Timothy? Someone you like? Or just Someone Who Lives In New York City Now?

Ok, now, wait. No! Ok! So, I *DO* hear your concerns (I do)— but the fact is that I can't fit this piece of furniture in my apartment anymore. And I'm really going to hold firm here. Ok? (Am I talking ... to myself ... in the third person ... in print? How terribly ... chic. ;)) Memories are memories, and I'll still have them regardless of my freaking furniture situation, so I hear your/my concerns, and maybe it is a little strange to sell something I've had for a long time, but I'm doing all of this with *love* and the *utmost* respect for this bookshelf. She's sperked so merch jer in mer lerf, but now it's time for her to sperk another kind of jer with ... I don't know. Someone else? Maybe some whole other purpose?

So, like, maybe, Craigslist shopper, you need, just, like, a plain, good, nice, utilitarian bookshelf? (And, again, I say all of those words with the *utmost* love and respect!) And this may be insane, but I'm going to call her a Gay Bookshelf, ok? And she is a survivor, honey! This bookshelf has survived moves between two Chicago apartments, a roadtrip all the way to New York City, and has had great, gay lives in two different NYC apartments over the years.

Oh, and people always mention pets in these ads, so, I *do* have dogs, but does that really matter for allergies when it comes to wooden furniture? Eh, just hose her off and pop a Claritin-D, queen! You'll be fine! Maybe you need a place to stack your books while you study for your PhD in Queer Studies! Maybe you need a plain backdrop where you can showcase your collection of geodes and crystals (omg I would love that for her)! Maybe you just need some spare wood.

But also, and not to get all "Giving Tree" about it, but maybe her life-cycle ends here. Maybe she's done her part, and maybe now she's meant to decompose. Maybe the universe needs her energy back again.

Omg. Typing that just gave me chills. How freaking poetic and beautiful is that thought, though? Chills!

Ok, so, here we go. New idea! How about this? If you need a FREE (I'm going to go back now and change the price to FREE) bookshelf and you promise that you'll give her a loving home (OR a loving purpose!), she's yours and I send her to her next journey with a lifetime of love and gratitude! She's been *just* the best to me, and I know you'll just love her. You can pick her up from my neighborhood in Astoria,

Queens, New York City, New York State, America! One flight of stairs, but I can lift her easily on my own, and I'm happy to help load her into your car for you.

And if no one emails by whenever this ad expires, well, then, maybe that's also the universe speaking. And if that's the case, she and I will *lovingly* part ways at the curb. A purpose well-served, and a partnership lovingly appreciated.

But, if you *do* want to offer me money for her, you will get *first* priority and maybe the highest bidder wins, too, ok? (I'm gonna go back and add "O/B/O," too.)

(And oh yeah, one more dumb thing, but my apartment is def haunted, BUT! I don't think she is. She doesn't SEEM to be haunted, at least. She seems normal, like a good, sturdy, happy, dependable bookshelf who's literally supported my things since before I had any things to speak of. But I promise you that I *will* sage her for you, if you want, so that you can have a fresh start with her. I think you'll really love her. She's a really great bookshelf.)

MyShelfMyself@gmail.com
Cash only.
Venmo is for str8s and Republicans.

HEALING

Maybe you've felt the creeping pressure to "love yourself" or practice "self-care," both worthwhile pursuits that can feel impossible precisely when you need them the most. Even those whose experiences have been relatively trauma-free (assuming those people exist) still carry battlescars from a lifetime on this Earth.

Healing doesn't necessarily look like spa treatments and rosé (though they can be helpful sometimes). It looks like a lot of ugly-crying, countless hours with very patient therapists, and probably too much time spent watching cooking competition shows. It's not fun. It's work. But it's worth it.

SHAPING UP

by Christian Luu

Full disclosure: the following essay contains frank discussion about disordered eating, body dysmorphia, self-harm, and suicidal ideation. If any of these are triggering for you, please proceed with your own health in mind. (Or don't! No judgment, babe.) Also, I'm literally not a doctor — sorry, Mom! — but I have been in a totally normal, not at all scary amount of counseling. This essay comes from my experience, as well as internet research, because it's 2019, and we be Googling.

I can say for a fact that one of the best episodes of *Full House* in terms of its depiction of contemporary issues and general heartfelt-ness, AS WELL AS being weirdly formative for me (a chubby Asian kid in the suburbs of Dallas, Texas), is the eighth episode of season four, "Shape Up," aka the episode where DJ Tanner, the OG BWB (Basic White Bitch) goes on a crash diet. To this day, every time I use a stationary bike, I think, "How many people would get the reference if I got off and just fainted on this sweaty gym floor?" If you haven't seen it, please feel free to put this down, stream it on Prime Video for $1.99 (LOL JK, it's 2019 and we be streaming illegally), and then come back when you've finished.

If you're hellbent on not falling down a *Full House* hole, I totally get it. Here's what you missed on *GLEE*!: Kimmy decides to have a pool party for her birthday (controversial, as we all know Kimmy has no friends except for the Tanner family). DJ, a 14-year-old inexplicably wearing a full face of makeup while flipping through off-brand magazines in her bedroom, grimaces at the idea because she feels her body doesn't compare to the bodies she's being bombarded with in the media.

Our heroine then embarks on an odyssey to achieve physical perfection in two short weeks. Obviously, everything she does to her body falls in line with symptoms of disordered eating. Still, we're directed to laugh when DJ pulls out an ice cube on a stick and calls it a "water pop" instead of having a piece of cake, which, of course, Michelle eats with her bare hands like a filthy, little animal. (The fact that the Olsen twins never received an Emmy nomination for their performance on this show is proof that white women are marginalized.)

They magically cure DJ's eating disorder by the end of the episode, and she manages to internalize body positivity in a five-minute conversation with her dad. Not my favorite representation of disordered eating on TV. (That award goes to *Degrassi: The Next Generation*, shoutout to Emma and Manny, the baddest bitches in the Toronto suburbs.)

The point is, that episode of *Full House*, while doing a great job of showing some of the thought patterns associated with disordered eating, also tells a dangerous lie: those of us who live with disordered eating patterns can be "fixed."

I'm not saying that if you have an eating disorder, you're cursed forever. HOWEVER, "health" and "progress" and "being normal" are all highly subjective, and it doesn't always happen for us the way it did for DJ. I thought there was something wrong with me because my story wasn't perfectly packaged with a bow and set to the roaring laughter of a studio audience like hers.

As a queer, Vietnamese-American kid growing up in a relatively traditional household, I first started hating my body when I got fat in the second grade. Why did I get fat in the second grade? Your guess is as good as mine. Maybe because Windows XP had just been released. Maybe because of 9/11. Maybe because I grew up in a house where our family related primarily through food, like a live-action version of Pixar's *Bao*.

I spent the next few years learning that my body was somehow incorrect, either through the media I consumed or through interactions with people who thought they were helping me by telling me I would be happier if I were skinny. The only thing that would probably change if I were skinny, is people would have stopped telling me how fat I was.

When I first started dancing at the ripe age of 19, my feet hurt like nobody's business. I thought it was normal, so I kept going, even though I was in an incredible amount of pain every class. One day, we were doing a very chill promenade in my ballet class. My feet hurt so much that I had to hold back tears while I was in the front row. My ballet teacher asked me what was going on, and I showed her my foot. It was so swollen it looked like a newborn baby's foot.

She was shocked, and I was like, "Oh, word? We're not all living this Hans Christian Andersen *Little Mermaid* life?"

We weren't.

I spent a week with my feet wrapped up with a medicine that made them go back down to normal size, and I got a pair of prescription insoles that made me feel like that scene in *Grey's Anatomy* where Dr. Hahn compares Dr. Calliope Torres' good-good püss to getting glasses. (So, it was like getting glasses, I guess. I just wanted to remind everyone of that iconic scene featuring Tony Award winner Sara Ramirez). I realized that my feet had always hurt like that. That's why I hated running. Everyone thought it was because I was fat and lazy, but actually I just had shitty feet. But now all of that was out the damn window! Dr. Hahn had nothing on me in these insoles, baby. I told my mom about that, and she said, "Yeah, but you should still try to lose weight or your feet will only get worse!"

Love that. Thanks, Mom.

I decided to go to undergrad in Oklahoma, because I couldn't afford to go to school in New York. I was still fat, but now had evolved into full-blown disordered eating. I was starving, binging, purging, restricting, self-harming, all while juggling a full class load. I'd also been out of the closet and sexually active for a few years, which meant I opened myself up to the glorious world of hook-up apps.

By now, we're all familiar with the "No Fats, No Fems, No Asians" rhetoric that persists in gay hookup culture today despite that banger from season eight *RuPaul's Drag Race* finalist Kim Chi. Look, I love racism, internalized homophobia and fatphobia as much as the next fat, queer, Vietnamese-American (not very much), but, the more the men in my life and online told me that my body wasn't worthy of sexual attraction, the more I tried to win them over by changing my body.

But here's the thing about my body: I will never look like a conventionally hot, cis, white, gay man.

So, with that knowledge, what did I do? Well, I had a couple of failed suicide attempts. I remember once in high school, I was in a really terrible mental place, and I wanted to kill myself by overdosing on gummy vitamins. HOWEVER,

Google said that was a bad idea because I would live and probably lose all of my hair ... so I didn't do that.

By this time, I knew what I was doing was wrong, but I didn't know if seeking help was the right thing for me to do. Mostly because I thought "help" would look like what I was used to. People who were "concerned" for my health because they thought I'd be "happier with less weight to carry around" actually encouraged my disordered eating habits. This happened a lot in college, mostly from professors. I think it's really interesting that they were never "concerned" for any of their students who binge drank and did cocaine on weekdays, but that's Not My Business™.

Whenever I told people about my experience with disordered eating, I would get a couple of reactions ranging from "Oh, you must have been bad at it because you're still fucking fat. Here are some MORE unsolicited tips for making your body skinny!" to "You're not fat, you're gorgeous!"

Here's what people who experience disordered eating patterns will tell you: both of these are capital G Garbáge things to say! The former reinforces the idea that the goal should still be a skinny body while shaming you for your disordered eating, and the latter implies that, in order to be considered beautiful, you have to be distanced from your fatness.

(If you're fat and someone says this to you, I dare you to say "Why can't I be fat AND beautiful?" and watch their head explode. Classic.)

It's interesting being a fat, queer person of color because people always treat me like I have a huge pimple on my nose that they're trying to politely ignore. I was having a late dinner once with friends, all of whom were conventionally hot, cis gay men who listen to Lizzo. We were drunk, obviously, and we ordered a TON of food. One of my friends off-handedly mentioned how much food it was, and how he was going to get *soooooo* fat. Then there was a moment when he realized what he said, thought he may have offended me, and did a very awkward Kellyanne Conway-style backpedal to acknowledge that he wasn't fatphobic. I said I didn't mind, because at that point I was already used to gaslighting myself to make other people comfortable, and then I went into the bathroom to throw up after the meal. It wasn't really the initial statement that triggered me, but more the way he made it clear that my fatness was shameful to mention in the first place.

I was talking to yet another conventionally-attractive cis gay friend (Should I Marie Kondo those????), and I told him about how a lot of gay spaces aren't made for me. Specifically, I was talking about the time I went to a sex party, and no one wanted to have sex with me. (True Story. RIP!!!!) Instead of laughing like I wanted him to, because it really was a funny story, he was like, "Hey, man. I totally get it. Not everyone is going to be attracted to you. Some people have said they don't like me because of my hair color."

He — let's call him (by his name), "Armie Hammer" — was completely obstinate to what I was actually saying. These spaces are made specifically to exclude me. You will never find me in Tom of Finland!!! I will not be featured in the next season of *American Horror Story*!!! I do not get invited to brunch!!!! This is all fine with me. (OK, the brunch thing is a little hurtful.) The point is that "Armie Hammer" was determined to filter my experience through his perspective, while completely disregarding my ACTUAL point. I ended up just agreeing with him, because that was easy at the time, and I really wanted to leave the conversation.

Do I just leave every conversation that I don't want to participate in? I mean, kinda. Healing is complicated and non-linear. I'm not sure if I'll ever be 100% the shiny and perfectly healthy version of myself that I want to be. At the time of writing this essay, it's been only one month since my last relapse. But, before that, I hadn't relapsed for almost two years, so, snaps for that.

Disordered eating, like many other mental illnesses, is like *The Babadook*, and not because it's so popular with queer people. It's like at the end of the movie, when that white lady has BabaDaddy locked in her basement and has to go down every so often to take care of it. Disordered eating is a part of my life, and I have to honor that. I have to work daily to manage my symptoms and avoid my triggers. It sucks because you never feel like you've really beaten it. Once you let yourself forget about it, it finds a way back into your life, like that weird internet game with the OK hand gesture.

One of the things that helps me deal with it all is having a queer support system that accepts everything about me. If I'm having a bad day, and I'm thinking about relapsing, I know I have people I can talk to who are nonjudgmental and unconditionally loving. If I have a relapse, I know my friends will hold me accountable while reminding me of what I already know — my disordered eating is not my fault, and I don't have to dwell on every mistake I make because of it. It's so empowering to surround yourself with people who understand you, who love you, who accept you as you are. I finally understand why rich, white people love the Greek system so much!

As someone coming from a Vietnamese-American house, this level of intimacy is really difficult for me. There are times when I don't feel like I deserve to be loved, and my instinct is to isolate myself. My logical brain knows that this is not what I really want, and it's not what my friends expect from me. I'm still learning how to accept affection, because honestly, it's a little overwhelming to have people in your life who love you when you don't love yourself. But being around all of the rad queer people in my life has done wonders for my mental health and self-esteem. 100/10 would recommend.

All the work doesn't come from my friends, although I'm sometimes inclined to believe it does. Objectively, I do a lot of work on learning to love my body. It's honestly done so much for me. I'm finally letting myself just BE, rather than trying to make myself conform.

In learning how to love myself, I've also learned that I'm nonbinary, which makes me feel like that scene in *Captain Marvel* where she realizes who she really is and can suddenly access her God-tier power. It's like that, except my power is reminding people that assigning gender to clothing is arbitrary, and we should stop doing it.

After my aforementioned relapse, I happened to re-watch the video of Cynthia Erivo singing "I'm Here" from *The Color Purple* (I beseech thee — look it up), and REALLY heard one line that made me burst into tears: "I believe I have, inside of me, everything that I need to live a bountiful life." Even though I had just lost two years of progress, that was the message that I needed to hear in order to keep going.

Everything I need is inside of me.

I am complete. I'm beautiful, and I'm here.

GOOD BONES

by Michael Foulk

For most of my life, I was terrified of penetrative sex. Honestly, all bodies, especially mine, seemed haunted, and my desires scared and perplexed me throughout my adolescence. Like, I was straight up frightened. Like, "We traced the call and it's coming from inside your body" spooked.

When I was in middle school, I became convinced that I was possessed by some sort of eldritch creature from another realm. I cycled through all the possible demons and spirits who might have been making a home out of my body. I would pour over books on mythology and religious iconography in my suburban Texas town's Round Rock Public Library on Main Street attempting to diagnose and identify the unwelcome squatter. This particular train of inquiry only lasted a short while but my body and what it wanted would continue to confuse me well into adulthood.

My issues with sex weren't for lack of interest — trust me, I was obsessed with the concept — but the whole to-do of it all disarmed me. Later in life, when I would try to submit myself to a sexual partner, my body would get all finicky and uncooperative like a water hose left too long with a kink in it. Nothing would work right. Every permutation of sex felt somehow wrong and impossible.

No one I knew had been able to teach me anything about the kind of sex I wanted to have — in fact, any and all information on gay sex had seemingly been erased from all of the books where I grew up. Little southern towns have a way of maintaining the whole extended moratorium on sodomy and all. I remember cherishing any sort of subversive media I could get my hands on. At 14, I thought *XY Magazine* was a radical piece of homosexual propaganda, and I was shocked that it was available in my local Hasting's. When I was finally able to dial-up-download pornographic photos, I stored them on floppy discs (six or seven low-res photos fit on each) and hid them in a KNEX box at the bottom of my closet with a pack of cigarettes and some old coins that my grandfather had given me.

When I first came out, I included a lot of caveats to my new identity. I swore up and down that I would never engage in penetrative sex on either end of the equation. I was going to keep it "Christian." You know, like Jesus and the apostles. Lots of mouth stuff but, you know, they were just friends. It was super important for me to place my gayness as close as possible to the heteronormative ideal as I could. I pulled that whole "I'm gay, but, like, that doesn't have to define me" schtick.

In my twenties, I had boyfriends, and I explored sex more, but every time it came to my body, to my penetration, I would lock up again. My defenses still engaged. I was unable to submit or participate. My brain, or at least part of it, was game but another part of me refused. Deep inside of me, it felt like something angry was lurking.

Supportive people have told me that there is no such thing as being "bad at sex;" there's only "bad sex" or "incompatible sexual partners," and intellectually I think I always understood that. But, emotionally, I truly felt as though I was the exception. Something was wrong with me. Something was broken inside of me. Even after I came out, I was sure that some part of me was rotten. My body felt haunted, unsafe, and inhospitable, like an old house full of Shirley Jackson spirits. I gave up. I put up a sign: DO NOT ENTER. My body was structurally unsound and prone to collapse. Abandon all hope ye who etc., etc. From a very early age, I felt condemned.

During this period of my life, I used to break into an old abandoned cotton mill in Walburg, Texas with my friends. The mill was straight out of a horror movie — literally portions of it were used as a filming location for the 2003 remake of *The Texas Chainsaw Massacre*. I'm not sure what happened to the mill that resulted in it shutting its doors and falling to rot, or why it was never torn down after all these years, but I suppose there is a story buried there. Something about small towns, money, and lost jobs.

This was during my "I'm not gay, I'm struggling with my sexuality" phase. We can translate that to "I still hook up with guys, but then I cry and pray about it afterward." I had already come out once when I was 15 but I sort of lost the thread of that identity when I started hooking up with older men that I met in AOL chat rooms. I wouldn't have "sex" with them but that wasn't because they didn't try. I became an expert at the dodge and weave, always offering an alternative, until one day I got too scared. A man drove me too far from my home on a road I didn't recognize and suddenly my mortality was very real. I put myself back in the closet, joined a youth church and got super religious. I wouldn't even attempt to have penetrative sex until I was 22 years old.

I was 19 at the time, living in Austin, and performing with a Christian screamo band then called The Kirby (later called Widows & Orphans ... it's still on Spotify). It was a whole moment. Think 2005. Think Chi Flatirons caked in hair product. Think Lucky Strike Cigarettes, lip rings, and women's jeans. I'm sure the era is conjuring some cringe-worthy images in your mind, and I would recommend you just apply them all. We were very invested in the contrived but earnest efforts we were making to define ourselves. I saw something in all of this posturing that I wanted.

I had joined The Kirby because I was functionally in love with one of the members of the band. In case you were wondering what to do if you have a crush on someone: DO NOT inexorably bind your life with that person for four years in hopes that they might eventually fall in love with you. They won't. I did all sorts of stupid unhealthy things while nursing this taboo crush. Drank to excess, drove unsafely. I dated a few very kind and understanding women while knowing deep down that I wasn't available in the way they were hoping. It was all dumb and unhealthy and very much standard for a closeted queer in their early twenties.

It was with these friends that I first broke into the abandoned cotton mill in Walburg. The mill was a massive, rusting two-story building with overgrown bushes and tall yellow grass surrounding it on all sides and blocking the facade from view. Inside, there was a central unit of "cotton machinery" that took up most of the interior space with a wrought iron maintenance catwalk surrounding the upper portion of the mass. The truss supporting the roof was failing and that loss of structural support had caused a cave-in on the south side of the building. This place was not safe to be wandering around in at night or any time of day but that made it way more exciting to explore. It was also a veritable spooky sound studio complete with clinking chains, moaning sheet metal, and dripping pipes.

Below the main machine unit, there was a stone stairwell that went down to a service basement where during our first visit to the mill we discovered a torn and soiled mattress. We were surprisingly undeterred, even though possibly bloody mattress is maybe No. 1 on the list of murderer-nearby red flags. We would come back to the mill often sporting flashlights and Lone Star Beer (in my opinion the best of the cheap beers) and just hang out. We had discovered our own shabby-chic condemned clubhouse.

One night, the guitar player and I went to the cotton mill in Walburg alone. Just the two of us with our flashlights and Lone Star. It was a date. It wasn't a date, but it had all of the trappings of a date. Or at least it was the closest thing to a date that I had experienced up to that point. We had returned to the mill many times over the years with more people without incident but on this particular mill trip, when it was just the two of us, something happened.

We parked our car to the left of the building behind some overgrown grass where we knew it couldn't be seen from the road. The guitar player and I walked up to the loading drive with our flashlights off to further hide our presence. We had never been caught sneaking into the mill before and we liked to believe that was because of our expert espionage skills. I set our standard issue six-pack of tallboys and my flashlight on the chest-high cement loading dock and hoisted myself up. We had been there enough times that we had a comfortable understanding of the layout of the mill without much light. The huge metal doors of the loading dock were rusted and covered in tags and vaguely religious graffiti. One piece I remember in particular featured the words "seven lives were washed in the blood of the lamb" and seven crudely scrawled white crosses. Standard murder mill stuff.

As we entered the mill, we heard a noise. It wasn't the clink of the chains or the wind that rustled the leaves on the tree limbs that had grown into the building through the hole in the roof. The sound was new and unnatural. It was a guttural and foreboding hiss that grew into a growl. And the sound got louder when we shined our flashlights near the maintenance crawl space. Yeah, the same space where we once had found a dirty torn mattress. Being the dumb, drunk, young men that we were, we decided to investigate further.

As we got closer, the sound intensified. We stepped through the threshold of a large wrought iron gate that separated the front section of the mill from the more mechanical rear, and then suddenly something huge rose up out the ground with a flurry of darkness and motion.

The nightmare creature landed on the iron grating around the machinery with a metallic thud and bellowed a blood curdling screech at us with its wings wide and imposing. It ran at us flapping it's massive five-and-a-half foot wings, the sound of its talons clanging against the hard rusting floor, its howl reverberating off the metal structure around us. We screamed and scrambled together back behind the iron gate we had passed through and slammed it closed just as the demon flew up to face-height to rip our eyes out. We fell to the ground and held the gate closed with our feet as the monster attacked. Eventually, after what seemed like an hour, but probably only amounted to a minute or two, the beast flew up through the hole in the roof, and we were left dirty, breathless, and bruised on the ground. We had just encountered an angry black vulture. We had disturbed its nest in the middle of the night.

I found myself thinking about this vulture a lot. It's screeching would come to mind when I thought of the guitar player and the one time we did finally kiss in a hotel room, the time when I knew he was just trying it because I had asked, just because he cared about me. Not in the way I was hoping. I would think about this vulture when I would try to have sex with future partners, when I would feel something angry and defensive rising up inside of me.

I would think about those men, too. The men I used to meet in AOL chat rooms. The men whom I had to repeatedly tell my boundaries, even as I was just learning what boundaries were; the men to whom I would offer alternatives, hoping that it would be enough to make them feel good, to make me feel real, to give my body value.

That vulture was just protecting its home. It had nested in that decaying mill, and it felt responsible for keeping away predators. It had no way of knowing what we intended to do, what kind of danger we posed. It just knew that it was scared that we wanted to take something away. It was afraid that we wanted to kill something that couldn't be brought back. I lived with a phantom version of this vulture inside the condemned wreck of my body for years; I convinced myself that it would always be there, screaming, refusing to let anyone enter.

Until one day it was gone. OK, fine. That's not true. That sort of oversimplification is a disservice to the truth. The real answer, the longer answer, the "Did this movie really need to be over two hours long?" answer is this: I spent well over a decade learning to trust people with my body, and I still struggle with it often. Too many men had tried to use me at too young an age, and no one had been able to teach me how to have a queer body in the first place.

Learning to let my guard down involved dozens upon dozens of attempts and a lot of disappointment. The first thing I had to understand was that I wouldn't break when someone was inside me. Despite all of my fears of the dismantled and decrepit interior structure of my body, I actually share little in common with the old forgotten mill I explored in my youth. I was just nervous, and I hadn't had an opportunity to feel strong yet.

Then it was a matter of finding sexual partners who knew how to read someone's body. I feel like pornography has convinced generations of men that every body is ready and waiting for them to dive into, and that is entirely and un-equivocally not the case. I was lowkey traumatized, despite talking a big game, and that needed to be taken into account when trying to engage in sexual activity. Sometimes during sex I would feel myself getting scared, angry, and defensive. Some sort of baggage from the fight-or-flight response was lingering in my subconscious. A large vulture, if you will. Sometimes during sex I would suddenly need to stop every-thing and relax. Sometimes I continued even though I felt tears boiling behind my eyes. Despite often feeling hopeless, I would always come back for another round of experimen-tation, and finally, at the age of 30, I was more or less fully able to let my guard down.

I know now that I was never condemned, I was just in an extended state of being remodeled. My body, or, more importantly, my mind, is in a good state now, though I'm still planning future refurbishments. The vulture has since retired and spends most of its time traveling. It still shows up every once in a while to water the plants, but usually it's out on a Royal Caribbean cruise or backpacking through Europe. Maybe the metaphor is dissolving.

What I mean to say is that vulture lived inside me for a reason, but, over time and with support from good folks, those reasons changed. It took me a long time to feel like my body was mine again after a lifetime of feeling unstable, unsafe, and afraid. I kept trying, and, eventually, I found a power in my body that I never knew I had before. I discovered just how sturdy I am. The vulture has moved on. My body isn't a haunted mill. It never really was. It's a cute brownstone with good bones.

To be real with you, it's actually kind of fancy.

SPECIAL (ARE YOU O)K CHALLENGE

by Danny Murphy

Due to my beautiful heritage as an Irish Catholic, my metabolism is slower than any Celine ballad. Weight has always been an issue for me. If Italians are affectionately known as stallions, I make the Irish look like *scallions* ... delicately placed upon a mound of buttery mashed potatoes. Not the kind of potatoes that operate as a small side dish, but rather a vehicle to ingest as much gravy, carbs, and whatever else can collect in the mini-mounds.

I can't act like I'm not at least partially to blame. Most of my youth was spent trying to create HTML codes for my MySpace profile page while deep-throating sleeve after sleeve of Oreos. This led to me having a face that looked like an entire DiGiorno pizza found a way to shove itself into a GAP cardigan. Nevertheless, I continued showing myself in public, which should have been seen as an act of courage on its own.

Two major shockers from high school: the first was that nobody bullied me despite me wearing an XL t-shirt from Lady Gaga's *Monster Ball* on multiple occasions, and the second? Being fifty pounds overweight weirdly will make you be your own bully. I scurried myself around freshmen and sophomore year, writing a column called *Gossip King* (truly, how was I not bullied?) and eating Fruit By The Foot by the mile. It's not that I haven't tried to diet in my life, I just didn't know how to do it correctly.

Slim Fast was something that was (and probably should have only been) consumed by single aunts in Boca Raton, Florida. I'm not sure how my greasy, middle school fingers got their hands on the first chocolate Slim Fast — I'm sure my mom, who also was blessed with a similar metabolism, bought it in an effort to actually diet properly. Well, however properly you can diet by means of a chocolate-flavored drink in a plastic bottle. After the first sip, I was hooked.

"This is good for me?!" I naively thought, in a way that younger siblings still believe in Santa, or like the way you right now think that guy who hasn't texted you in a week-and-a-half is just 'busy with work.' It's okay, we all have those moments. After all, I'd say my relationship with Slim Fast wasn't unlike a summer fling — we hit hard and fast, and it ended with me crying on a toilet, shitting out my entire life. I think the moment I knew it was officially over between me and Slim Fast was when I debated bringing a can of it to a friend's pizza party. Pizza always wins, and sometimes, so does just being a kid. I haven't touched the stuff since, cold turkey style, but every now and then I still remember the coated feeling my tongue would get after hooking back a bottle (or two).

I wasn't just trying to lose weight one milkshake at a time. The summer before my senior year, I had a little more free will, but just as little self-esteem, so I did what every young homosexual with body issues and a gently used sedan would do: I joined a gym. And, with that, I immediately started getting the smiles and nods people who aren't fit get from the attractive people in a gym. It's sort of the same smile you give to someone who you know is going to the floor of your office that is exclusively for getting laid off. It's compassion, but it's mainly pity and an overwhelming sense of relief because they're not you.

It was there I learned I'm great at a lot of steps leading up to a workout. An inspiring, fun playlist? Mine is nine hours. A snack in the car for 'protein replenishing' or whatever phrase I'm making up to justify a snack? On deck. Hell, I'm even phenomenal at going to the gym and walking around. I can walk circles around any weight machine, looking like a vulture waiting to strike whatever exercise I'm going to make my bitch, when in reality I'm just thinking about what celebrity should be ripped apart next in my school's paper. I mean, it's hard to get a strenuous workout in when you're carrying the weight of the *Gossip King* crown.

Here's where I found my exercise calling, however: the elliptical. I'm sure you can get a legitimate workout on an elliptical, but when you're with me, you're not part of the resistance — at most, your resistance is at a 2. So, I started with the elliptical and would just walk on it for 30 minutes, which, let's be honest, made me about as good at working out as Real Housewives are at launching clothing lines.

Now I want you to visualize who was riding on this trip: an acne-ridden, Lady Gaga XL shirt wearing 16 year old. Summer plans? Not that many. Weird no one wanted to listen to me quote *Funny Girl* while they drink Natural Light in the woods — a fact that hasn't changed, unfortunately. Because of this, I really didn't do anything during the summer besides watch *Ghost Whisperer* and go to the gym. The result? Gasp! I was fitting in jeans from actual stores. I felt great, and as lord-and-savior Britney Spears said best, "Gimme more."

The more, obviously had to come from the 'diet' portion of 'diet and exercise.' I was a vegetarian since the sixth grade due to a personal New Year's Resolution I made to myself while counting down to midnight in some West Virginian hotel with a family whose last name was Bird. (All their nicknames were like, colors, so the youngest girl was Blue Bird — a fact I hated immediately even as a teen, proving I've always been a slight cunt. It's my rising moon sign, after all).

I wasn't going to cook, because I've only turned a stove on maybe seven times in my entire life. More importantly, I wasn't going to learn what 'paleo' meant — this was before Instagram was in its prime and everyone was hashtagging the fact they eat like a caveman. This journey led me to the grocery store with my mom, a task I used to hate doing, which is weird because now grocery stores are in my Top 3 favorite places to loiter when I'm nervously early to any event. So, I would help with the shopping while looking for anything that could potentially give me the body of … someone that wasn't me. Healthy!

I ended up in the cereal aisle, an aisle that I think is never associated with health. To be honest, growing up I wasn't a major Cereal Head. (I also never got into *Serial* the podcast either — so TBD if there's any connection until Sarah Koenig cracks this case.) My breakfasts, like my personality, would always lean on the warmer side (right?), like a warm Toaster Strudel or two. One of my classic pre-school breakfasts was two Toaster Strudels and a Redbull & OJ. Basically, I was a mix between Honey Boo Boo and a semi-functioning alcoholic.

But, then, I saw the phrase: Special K Challenge. It was surrounded by a depiction of measuring tape cinching the words, indicating that, yes, all of the letters in 'Special K

Challenge' are at their goal weight and in functional relationships. I desperately wanted to be part of that world. I grabbed two boxes. Naturally, the ones I grabbed were the chocolate flavor, because baby steps. And then my journey began.

The Special K Challenge also sounds like something that should only exist for aunts, but this time, aunts in, like, Rhode Island. It's less of a diet and more of a 'challenge,' meaning you're supposed to do it and move on from it. Kind of like that phase in your monogamous relationship when you do a threesome to spice up your life, but then you delete your couple's Tinder in a week because you realize the real void in your relationship was an HBOGo login. But, much like MTV's show *The Challenge*, this went on much longer than expected or desired.

Turns out, The Special K Challenge isn't for aunts, but rather it's for the secretary at your mom's office who's divorced but hopeful: swiping on Tinder while getting ready for her cardio dance class at Crunch gym. It's for the person who just wants a drastic life change after getting hit with rejection and failure time after time. Basically, my energy. I took to this challenge the way Roxanne Gay-reading, intersectional feminists from small conservative towns in the Bible Belt took to a brochure for Vassar College in their guidance counselor's office: as an only hope.

Can I be honest? I killed the Special K Challenge game. Cereal with chocolate pieces for breakfast? Yeah, girl, I'm into it. Throw on some Unsweetened Vanilla Almond Milk, because I have always been that bitch in front of you at Starbucks, and you got a new lifestyle. It's awesome too because you can have snacks, and by snacks I mean Special K bars or a banana. My excitement over this fact goes to show just how quickly I could be brainwashed into joining a cult.

I was cocky that summer. I would talk to literally no one. (I'd say it was because I was in the zone, but mainly because, although I wasn't bullied, it didn't mean I had a Rolodex of friends to watch *Friends* with.) All I would do was wake up, Special K, watch five hours of *The Ghost Whisperer,* Special K. This would be followed by me Googling "how to get a Disney original series" and then going to the gym to elliptical until my heart rate was deemed 'healthy' by the Fat Burner setting.

Three months later, I had a waist. What a twist! The best compliment I received was from a gym employee, who while I was filling up my water bottle told me: "You've lost weight, but your stomach is naturally fat. You need to do more abs and weight-lifting." Hello, soulmate! After shockingly not getting arrested for murder, I prepared myself for my first day of school. Turns out, spending the summer eating only cereal does wonders for fast weight loss — and hey, they just released a new flavor called Vanilla Almond, so I was ready to ride the Special K train straight to graduation.

I went to school with a packed lunch, including what I thought was a very chic cereal holder that sort of ended up looking like something from Zelda. I'm only assuming what 'something from Zelda' would look like, because, despite my acne, I managed to convince myself I was actually too cool to play.

The actual best compliment came from my choir teacher. When we went around the room saying what we did that summer, he looked right at me. In that moment, I thought he was going to ask why I chose to continue doing the class despite lip-syncing every performance (does he not know how pop stars are born?), but instead he congratulated me on all the weight I had lost. I'm not sure if that is taught in the courses you need to be a choir instructor, but comments about a student's weight do fun things to their heads! That was the feedback I always wanted. In that moment, being called thin felt as exhilarating as when your square buzzer from Panera Bread goes off when your sandwich-soup-with-chips-and-yes-more-bread is ready.

After a few months into the school year, though, I realized, hmm, maybe I do want to try a workout more intense than a Key West Retirement Plan. So, the next time I went to the gym, I tried to lift weights and realized I had no strength. Like, so little strength that I couldn't have even lifted the fake weights in Olivia Newton-John's *Physical* music video. I'd been working out and dieting for months! Why didn't my body want to be the hot body it deserved to be? It was then I realized that I had been treating my body like Jennifer Lopez's character in the first half of *Enough*, and it was time to turn into Jennifer Lopez's character from the second half of *Enough*. I walked right into the high school trap of wanting to be thin, because I wanted to be accepted. I wanted to be the kid who could confidently go into J. Crew, not the kid who had to order the only size that fit them online from J. Crew, which, believe me, is no way to live at all.

So, I poured all my Special K cereal boxes out. Just kidding, I'm not that wasteful, bitch. I still had it for breakfast, with blueberries in it, because *Goop* told me it would be good for me. And by now you know that if it's good enough for Gwyneth Paltrow, it's definitely good enough for me.

But, I ended my extended challenge and started a different challenge that I am still working on: treating my body with respect. And, unfortunately, there's no cheat codes for that on the back of cereal boxes (yes, not even the weird ones with flax seed). Rather, that's a challenge I face every day.

There's no magical switch that will make you fall in love with your body overnight — instead, it's a slow burn process that more often than not involves a Barre class. Learning to treat the skin you're in with respect is an important relationship for everyone to take on, because you never know when the dressing room at Zara can become a war zone, or when a relative's comment about how much food is on your plate at Thanksgiving can strike next.

Little do they know, this Irish scallion is stronger than the plate his seconds of mashed potatoes are placed on.

SUNLIGHT

After practicing hiding parts of ourselves for so long, it takes time to unlearn the little tricks we've picked up along the way to keep ourselves safe, our livelihoods secure, and to get our parents to stop asking if we hold hands with our partners in public, MOM.

We receive so many messages — some loud and intentional, many well-meaning but just as difficult — to hide parts of ourselves. It's scary stepping out into the sun. Sometimes, even within the queer community and queer spaces, it's still a struggle to feel like you fit in. But every time you show up as your authentic self, you make it a little easier for the next person.

The next few authors have taken that step, and I hope you're ready to follow.

Just don't forget the SPF.

CHOOSING AUTHENTICITY

by Dubbs Weinblatt

"It's a girl," the doctor exclaimed on December 12th, 1984. After taking a quick glance at my body, the doctor not only assigned my sex* but also my gender identity**. Based on this designation, my parents knew the exact prescription to raise a little girl who fits into society's tidy, little box.

Like most of us, I'm not always tidy. And I don't like little boxes.

Starting from as early as I can remember, I knew I was different. And I knew I had to hide it, and I couldn't talk about any of it. I looked around, saw families and knew I wanted one, but I also knew that mine would look different. I saw adult men and women, and felt a disconnect from them. I had no idea what any of it meant, but I knew it was wrong.

Any time anyone would say negative things about queer people: faggot, faygala (Yiddish slang for faggot), he/she, that 'thing' (said with venom), etc., I'd mentally write a note to myself and file it away in my brain. I quickly learned that to veer away from 'the norm' was a dangerous path, and I'd best stay the course.

I felt most comfortable hanging with the boys. I chose Umbros over skirts, and t-shirts over blouses every.single. time. The older I got, the harder it became to stay true to myself, and the more I felt like I needed to conform to survive.

It became more real when I started to recognize my feelings were different than most of my peers. My classmates began to care more about impressing the boys than hanging with each other or playing outside. My days were filled with fantasies of the girls crushing on ME and what that world would look like. I dreamed about a world where this was normal and I could tell my friends who I actually had a crush on instead of lying about being in love with the least-threatening, Jewish boy that wasn't claimed.

One aspect of my identity that was always very important to me was my Judaism. Even though I didn't see myself reflected anywhere in our tradition (even though queer people *are there)* or in the very fabric that made us who we were, I felt drawn to the community and the specialness I felt that came with being a Jew. We had summer camp where you could be your true self. We had eight nights of presents at Channukah. As a 12-year-old, that's about all that mattered to me, Jewishly, that is.

Besides the whole refusing to let Rabbis marry people of the same gender thing, I kind of liked being Jewish until it was time for my Bat Mitzvah. In Judaism, this is when a young girl becomes a woman in her family's and community's eyes. I didn't *want* to become a woman. I didn't *want* the 'girls' gift from our Sisterhood (girls got Shabbat candlestick holders, and the boys got wine glasses — why couldn't every kid just get all the things?). I didn't *want* to go to my party and have to pick a boy to dance with during the Snowball dance in front of everyone. I just wanted the popcorn and the presents and to call it a day. I didn't want any of it. But I did it, because that's what nice, Jewish girls do. I didn't want to disappoint my parents or my community.

Plus, the party and all the presents sounded *okay.*

I think back to some of the other Bar/Bat Mitzvah parties that I attended, and what I remember is truly wild. At some of them, we could stick our hands in a bucket of ice for a few minutes until they were completely numb, dip our hands in lotion, make some kind of gesture, and then stick it in burning hot, liquid wax to form some kind of 'take home treasure' after the wax cooled. We were banned from throwing up the middle finger, so the next best options were either a peace sign or 'the shocker' (even though none of us would know what that was for a few years). I always opted for the peace sign, but sadly no longer own any of those beautiful memories.

Or what about the photobooths and endless buffets and live bands and personalized t-shirts and scrubs and slippers and hats and cotton candy and ice cream and privilege dripping out of every corner of these things?

If you think you've seen it all on *My Super Sweet Sixteen*, just wait until you've marathon-watched a lifetime of *My Magical Mitzvah*.

I digress.

It was November 14th, 1997, the day before my fate would be sealed as a brand-new woman, and my parents and I were in the parking lot of Temple Israel on East Broad Street in Columbus, Ohio. We had just left my final dress rehearsal before the main event.

"Mom, please, I don't want to have a Bat Mitzvah," I pleaded.

"Give me one good reason why!"

Oh, I had plenty of reasons: "I don't want to wear a skirt. I don't want to wear tights. I hate wearing my hair down." But the one reason I was still not ready to give was the most important one: I DON'T WANT TO BECOME A WOMAN. I didn't know that was something I could say, let alone feel. I didn't know that was already my truth.

The next morning, I rushed to get dressed so we could get the show on the road and get it over with. I threw on my gray, plaid wool skirt/kilt (why, Mom, why?), white turtleneck (it was the '90s!), black fleece vest (again, why, Mom, why), my tights and these really sick black flats (not in a cool way, they actually looked unhealthy). My hair was down, and I was ready to play my part in the award-winning show I was about to put on.

Betwixt reading Torah and being blessed into woman-hood in front of a house of 200 plus family, friends, and fans, I turned to my mom and whispered, "I FORGOT DEODORANT!"

Told you I wasn't tidy.

As my mother ushered me to the podium to receive my fate and give my acceptance speech, I blacked out. I don't remember my d'var Torah, or as the non-Jews call it, "the speech," or my party really at all. I have pictures that show I danced with Jonah Rothstein and David Finkelstein and that I wore a big, foam finger. Other than that, I remember jack squat except all the paper gift certificates to Media Play and Gap Kids.

I kept thinking to myself that life was just going to keep getting harder, and I'd have to keep suppressing more and more the older I got. I thought the reasons for my unhappiness all had to do with me being gay; I had no idea there were gender demons lurking about.

When I got to high school, life had already gotten really hard. My hormones were raging, and I was all alone. I couldn't share with my friends or family what was going on because I was terrified I'd lose them. I still hadn't really had any positive experiences with seeing queer people in my sphere.

I felt so much pain from not being able to share my thoughts with anyone in my life. I started a million journals to try and just get it all out of me, but I was terrified someone would find them, so I never put to paper anything I was feeling. It was all bottled up inside and starting to take a toll.

The summer going into my sophomore year of high school, I went to a house party where I had my first taste of alcohol. I was 14 years old. I loved every drop I drank. I loved the feeling of escaping reality and numbing the pain and hurt that I felt every minute of every day. Drinking gave me the sense of control I didn't have in my life otherwise. And the after-effects of drinking were just as great. Not remembering most of the night was ideal. I subconsciously was using drinking as an excuse not to be held accountable and erasing big parts of my life.

My alcohol consumption increased as I made my way through high school, and, after I started college at Ohio State, it only worsened. Day drinking was encouraged. Happy hour deals ruled my life.

At that point, I only knew of one or two gay people, and they always made disparaging comments about lesbians. I felt more and more alone every day.

Each time I drank, I became more angry and upset. I developed an alter-ego named Brevrick that lashed out each time I drank. I was starting to really drive a wedge between myself and my friends. I was feeling more and more hopeless that I would never get to be myself.

One night while I was drinking alone in my room during sophomore year of college, my best friend knocked on my door and gave me an ultimatum: "You drink too much, and I can't keep taking care of you. Either tell me what's going on or we can't be friends anymore."

That was my moment of truth. I had to decide if it was worth me risking it all by coming out. I was too scared to say it out loud, so I took a post-it and wrote 'I'm Bi' on it. To me, that was the easier route than gay because it was giving myself an out if I needed it. I think a lot of queer people actually initially come out as bi, because it's hard to commit to one identity, to one tidy box.

I thought once I came out things would be different. I thought I'd be able to handle my alcohol. I thought I'd start dating women immediately, but it actually turned out none of those things were true. I tried on different labels like bi, gay, lesbian, but the only one that really seemed to fit was gay.

My drinking only worsened, and I sabotaged any and every chance I had with the girls I was dating. There was something else deep inside me that was plaguing me. I no longer had suicidal ideations and was generally happier, but there was a cloud of inauthenticity looming that I couldn't quite figure out.

I moved to NYC in the summer of 2011, and my life started to change. I invested all of my time and money in improv classes, teams, and shows, and I made a whole new group of friends. I explored the city with my old friends and new, and started to learn about all different kinds of people. A few years later, I went to a 'Lipstick Lesbian Awareness Party' in the Lower East Side during Pride month, and my life was forever changed. I entered the party already feeling a little out of place, because at that point I didn't identify as a lesbian (and definitely not a lipstick one).

All of a sudden, I had a glass-shattering, a-ha moment. I didn't fit in there because not only was I not a lesbian, I was not a woman. I realized that I felt no connection to and hated my given name. I hated the way my messenger bag fit across my chest. I hated my chest. I just didn't know what it all meant.

The only trans people I knew existed were binary trans people; those who are trans men or trans women. When I thought about the possibility of being trans, I was scared because I didn't feel like I was a man.

I had no idea there were genderqueer/non-binary identities.

I decided almost immediately in that moment that I wanted, nay, needed to have Top Surgery (a double mastectomy where both breasts are removed in a major surgery). The second I made this decision, I felt lighter. I felt more like myself than ever. I changed my name to something that was more me. I was debating taking hormones, but that never felt right to me. I didn't know anyone else who had Top Surgery but wasn't on hormones and wasn't a trans man. I felt really alone, but I also knew this was the right thing for me.

After months of trying to find a doctor that would see me (as a non-cancer, non-binary trans patient) and then fighting with insurance, I finally scheduled my surgery two years later. Almost immediately my drinking started lessening and lessening. I could feel my whole body relaxing.

Once the surgery was over, I truly felt like a different person. I felt more myself than I'd ever felt. When I looked in the mirror, I actually saw ME. I had no idea what I was missing.

It's scary choosing to be authentic. And, yes, authenticity is a choice. Every day I decide to show up as my true self. And it's not always easy. When you show up as your full self and people reject you, it hurts a little deeper because it's not a shell or a facade they're rejecting, it's you at your core. However, I found once I started living in a way that was authentic for me, things started falling into place.

I connect to myself and my body in ways I never knew were possible. When people ask me how I am, I actually mean it when I say I'm great. I finally have the energy to date people in a real way. I started making moves in my career because I finally felt like I deserved it. My whole life was built on the assumption that I was a failure because I never really felt like myself, and I never cared about my future or my career because it wasn't really mine. After my surgery and after I started identifying in a way that was authentic for me, all of that changed.

I wonder how different my life would have turned out if I would have known from the start that I didn't have to become a woman or that non-binary gender identities existed. Or that I didn't need to take hormones to be a trans person or that I could have Top Surgery, because it was the right decision for me and not just a box to check off for a Trans Man's journey. It's all about that visibility, baby! So now that I'm living my truth, loud and proud, I hope I can show other folks who may be struggling with their identities all the possibilities that exist for them.

Imagine how empowered we'd all be if we knew from the start all of the different choices we had to affirm who we are; even if they're the more vulnerable choice — the one that goes against the grain. When we choose to live more authentically, the highs are higher and the lows are lower and it's worth it and I'd never choose to live any other way.

sex assigned at birth: a designation based on primary, external sex characteristics.

gender identity: an internal sense of self and understanding of who you are and how you relate to the world. No one can determine your true gender identity, only you can.

BEARLY THERE

by Danny Artese

Well before Robyn's perfect album *Body Talk*, my body had a lot of things to say to me that I didn't think the other boys' bodies were telling them. As early as 3 years old, mine told me that it was more interested in first position than first base. In elementary school, my body was fine with jungle gym X-Men battles, but it wanted to conjure the wind and rain as Storm while the other boys brandished Wolverine's claws or Cyclops's laser beams. In math class, I was more interested in observing the differences between Tyler and Billy than between squares and rectangles. It wasn't until sixth grade that a family friend mentioned his male significant other, which I'd never heard of before, and my brain caught up to my body.

My "questioning" phase lasted about as long as it took for AOL to dial up and for me to search, verbatim, "Am I gay?"

I think I beat Ellen coming out by a few months, and I sought out any other relevant media I could find. Obviously, I started my self-imposed gay curriculum by watching black-and-white films starring every single person in Madonna's Vogue "rap" (Greta Garbo and Monroe, Dietrich and DiMaggio — not an actor, it turns out). I graduated to '90s teenage indie classics like *Beautiful Thing* and *But I'm a Cheerleader*, with general ed courses in *XY Magazine*, that cowboy calendar at the Calendar Club pop-up in the mall and a certificate program in seeing *Rent* on tour and wearing out the soundtrack CD. Available movies and TV revealed a pattern: teenagers coming of age could be loners in their small towns with just that one special someone with whom to share being gay. But once they were adults, they headed to bigger cities to find their tribe. From *The Broken Hearts Club* (hi, gay Superman) to *Queer as Folk*, beautiful gay men found a group of other beautiful gay men to exist within. This perceived homosexual desirability caste system was super helpful if you looked like a Hollywood hunk, but not so much if you looked like me.

So instead of my body telling me things, it just asked me a question: Where do I fit in?

Adolescent me was 5'7" and 170 pounds, fair but tan-looking next to the gothier of my friends, with acne mostly taken care of by ProActiv. I had thick, curly hair that I could brush into a disco marshmallow halo or gel into ramen-noodle submission that would make Justin Timberlake blush. One time, I tried dying my hair a rich chocolate brown, thinking that it would make my light eyes pop and somehow also thinking that it would make my hair sleek and sexy. Did you know that dark brown hair can be just as frizzy as dark blond hair?

I had some good ideas about what I wasn't, but struggled to figure out what I was. I wasn't tall, but I wasn't a pocket gay, a term I heard once on *Will & Grace*. I wore anywhere from a 31 to a 33 waist, depending on the brand. I wasn't skinny, but I certainly didn't have abs. I wasn't fat, but my torso was more H-shaped than V-shaped. I took dance classes, and I had a butt; but the idea that my chest could ever protrude beyond my stomach was laughable. I was the first in my grade to sprout a happy trail, but I'm still waiting for a fifth facial hair to show up today.

I developed a technique to change T-shirts in P.E. class without ever showing my body, and, let me tell you, Jennifer Beals could never. I didn't think I was ugly or *un*attractive. I just figured that if anyone was describing me to a potential suitor, it would end with: "and he's got a really fun personality!" In my America Online continuing studies class, I learned some basic gay taxonomy: twinks, bears, and otters. My eye was particularly drawn toward the Bear genus, and I learned there were subspecies like cubs, polar bears, muscle bears, and leather bears. Each unique, but generally all beefy, beardy, and covered with body hair. I had none of the three Bs. I felt like my body was just ... there.

My high school in suburban southern California was a queer desert without any other out prospects, so I would have to wait until I moved to the big city after graduation to learn my place. In college (but not *in college*), I learned that bears were just the beginning; there were pups and piggies and wolves, oh my. But there were also theater queens, musical theater queens, drag queens, circuit boys, activists, gay nerds, fashion gays, and more that had nothing to do with appearance. And yet, in this choose-your-own-adventure, I still didn't know which page to turn to! Where was my clique? Who would want to hang out with me? Most importantly, in my 19-year-old wisdom, who would think I was hot? I was most attracted to bearish types, so I figured that was who I most wanted to be attracted to me, but I had an average build, an inability to grow facial hair, and an aversion to plaid. The bear community was a party to which I could never be invited.

Being 21 in New York City gave me the ability to go to bars and clubs, but I didn't because I hadn't figured out my "scene" yet. (Also, because D.A.R.E. had been very effective in my youth.) In the quaint days before Grindr, I thought of bars as just places that guys went to find hookups with similarly attractive guys. But I wasn't worried about with whom I'd leave these specific, specialized microsocieties; I was worried if they'd let me in the door in the first place.

Then, by chance at a friend's Halloween gathering, I met the first guy with whom I would make it beyond a second date. That night, I was dressed as Nemo, and he was dressed as a fisherman, so he … found me. Maybe I subconsciously dressed as a fish swimming upstream in an attempt to attract a grizzly, but a fisherman would do!

Unfortunately, I didn't even realize his standing close and barely talking to anyone else the whole night indicated we were hitting it off that way until the next day when our mutual friend insisted that he was interested in me. The signs were so foreign to me that I didn't see them.

The validation of strangers is one thing, but your first boyfriend, the first man to tell you he loves you, with whom you live in a cozy studio apartment, is really something else. Studio apartment is another word for zero-bedroom. I had to be careful getting out of bed so I didn't bump into the refrigerator, and the only door other than the front door was to the bathroom, if either of us needed a moment alone.

In our two and a half years together, I gained precious memories, some wisdom about what I did and didn't want for myself, and a little over 30 pounds. I looked less like those Hollywood hunks than ever, but for the first time I felt like my body wasn't just *there*. It might be described as thicc, husky, or chubby depending who you asked, but at least descriptors existed. Sure, my body wasn't everybody's cup of tea, but it hadn't been when I was thinner, either. Besides, some people prefer a little extra something in their tea. Like honey. And you draw more bears with honey than vinegar. What's that about bees? No, no, I'm pretty sure it's bears.

We broke up in April, and he moved out in June. (Side note: I do not recommend continuing to live with your first boyfriend in a cozy studio apartment for three months after you break up. Emotionally, we couldn't afford to stay, but financially neither of us could afford to leave.) The last weekend in June is Pride and also usually my birthday weekend. Coincidence? When I looked up the parade route and start time leading up to that Sunday, a banner ad alerted me to an after-Pride bear dance party being held at Webster Hall, a concert venue downtown. I Googled the capacity of the space and learned it could hold 1,400. *One thousand four hundred bears under one roof?* Out of curiosity, I clicked the link to learn more and found out it was billed as a "masked ball." "Mask for mask" jokes aside, the fact that there would actually be masks struck me as perfectly ridiculous. The bears wouldn't even be able to see each other, just anonymously judge each other based on their bodies. It would be like the internet IRL! But I could go without telling anyone I knew and then hide in plain sight!

I could try on being a bear for a day.

I surprised myself and bought a ticket.

My body was closer to cubbishness than it had ever been, and I wondered if there might in fact be a place for me in a bear-meet-bear world. I still didn't have a beard or more than a sprinkling of body hair, but one out of three Bs ain't bad! Over the next few days, I went back and forth between definitely going and deciding it was too preposterous. I was terrified of any of my friends finding out I was considering this. In reality, if I had told any of my friends that I was thinking of going, they probably just would have said, "Sounds fun; have a good time!" but in my mind I thought they would encircle me and stretch to 12 feet tall while they laughed at my thinking I could even possibly be included. So I kept my mouth shut and got a mask at Party City, just in case.

I got home from the parade still undecided about that night's plans. Since no one knew I had a ticket, no one but me would know if I didn't use it. Or if I did. After a late dinner, I showered to rinse off the sweat and any remaining sunscreen from standing outside all afternoon. I am not a naked person. I do not walk around my apartment naked, and I get very concerned about sitting on just about any surface in my home without a layer of fabric between us. So after my shower, I needed to put *something* on. It could either be pajama pants and a baggy t-shirt or ... those dark blue jeans I liked to think made me look good from the back and a tank top. But not a black tank top, because black tank tops are for people who think they look good in tank tops. And not a white one, because that would look too much like an undergarment. So an exact compromise: grey ... with a casual button-down over it for the subway ride. I do not know why I owned three tank tops. I had never worn even one of them before this night.

I boarded the train from Queens to downtown Manhattan, and for the first time in my life I hoped for delays. Signal problems! Train traffic ahead of us! Carrie Bradshaw on the tracks unable to help herself from wondering! Maybe I'd get lucky and there would be a violently sick passenger! Alas, I arrived at Union Square on schedule. I could get right back on an uptown train and head home for an early night's sleep, or I could march up to the front door and stake a place for myself, even if just for a night.

My mask stayed firmly in-hand when I entered Webster Hall in case it was lame and no one was wearing one. Stepping into the two-story dance floor like Dorothy after the tornado, but without the benefit of sudden Technicolor, it turned out my concerns were a little misplaced.

Not only was no one wearing a mask; no one was … *there.*

The dance floor was empty except for one guy off to the side clearly enjoying whatever non-D.A.R.E.-approved substance he'd ingested. There were exactly two guys at the bar. I walked around the edges of the dance floor in case the event wasn't on the main floor, but I only found two more guys in a tiny side lounge, very aggressively thumb-wrestling (based on the sounds I heard through the doorway as I scuttled away). The mezzanine was closed off, so no one was up there. My arrival had brought the grand total of attendees to six. I guess the good news was that I was in, and there were no cliques to contend with. I checked my flip phone: it was a little after 10 p.m. Maybe the other 1394 bears would arrive at 11?

By 11 p.m., not a single additional attendee had shown up, but a band had taken the stage. I stood front and center in the audience like I would at a concert, clapping loudly after each song. As an artist, I somehow imagine it would be sadder to perform for an audience of one than to an empty room. When the band finished their set around midnight and DJ music took over, nobody else had arrived. Bears at 1 a.m.? I don't know why I thought everything happened on the hour. I killed time looking at posters for upcoming shows, going to the bathroom without needing to go to the bathroom, and checking repeatedly for voicemails I might have missed. 1 a.m. came and went, and we still had not made it past four of us on the main floor. I decided I had made a valiant effort, and it was time to go home.

I had survived my entry into the bears' den. I was enormously let down but relieved on my way to the exit. I will never know why the event wasn't cancelled. As I neared the lobby door to leave, I recognized the opening notes of a Robyn song I loved and wasn't sure whether to leave or turn around.

Like a Muggle desperately hoping for a Hogwarts letter that would never come, I had been waiting years for my official invitation to join the bear party until the loophole presented itself that night: a disguise. Yes, I literally had bought my way in, but *figuratively* I snuck in a side door. I had so agonized over whether the tank top under my button-down was acceptable dress code in that world and whether anyone else would be wearing masks, that it never occurred to me to worry whether anyone else would even show up. And after all that I had built up that event to be, nobody was there. No bear high council to permit or deny entry. No cliques of cute cubs to rush to join. Nobody.

In addition to her songs, my favorite thing about Robyn is that she left her label and started her own so she could do what she wanted to do. As for me, I started the night wanting 3 things: to get in the door, to take up (a little extra) space in this previously off-limits world, and to dance. I had accomplished the first, and the other two didn't actually require anyone else's permission or presence like I thought.

So, sure, I could go home and get a decent night's sleep and pretend the night never happened. Or I could head back to the dance floor and finally take off my overshirt because it was hot and I'd picked just the right tank top. Plus, it was

Pride, it was my actual birthday and my ass looked great in my 36s.

I had a hundred feet of clearance in all directions, and I could truly start dancing on my own.

GYM, DYKE, LAUNDRY: 8 QUEER COMMANDMENTS TO HELP YOU GET BACK INTO THE GYM

by Lorena Russi

I grew up in Queens with a family of Colombian immigrants who clouded sex and sexuality in secrecy. It goes without saying, coming out to my family was difficult. But coming out to my second family of teammates and queerdos was even harder. In terms of queerness, immigrants and athletes share a 'don't ask, don't tell' mentality. And while, conversely, LGBTQ spaces have open arms, as a community, I couldn't come out to them as an athlete without isolating others or myself. Namely, because sports are heteronormative spaces that are triggering as all fuck for a lot of queers. It took decades for my "Queer" and "Athlete" identities to coexist harmoniously.

In fact, I did my best to separate them, despite the fact that they were siblings of the same womb. Athletes were scared of the dyke in the locker room, and queers were scared of the insensitive jock with the rainbow flag. As a result, I did my best never to let the two mix, except for the only space where it was inevitable. Where's that, Lorena? Well, my children, it's where cis-het males go to roam freely: the weight room. Like Jonah, I found myself in the belly of the whale ... except the belly was a room full of men lifting kettlebells.

In the weight room, I was extremely vulnerable. Against huge, veiny Davids and Eriks, I was weaponless. I couldn't use comedy as a defense mechanism because no one talks to each other. I wasn't strong enough to impress them with my athletic skills. And I couldn't even use my body to distract them, because they were definitely not attracted to me (my buzz cut and below the knee shorts screamed "homo" with each deadlift). At the gym, the only tool I had was embarrassment; because, being there as a Queer Athlete meant I was existing as my truest self. And I was ashamed of that person. I watched 200lb men in napkin-thin tank-tops scarf down protein shakes and WHOOP after sets, and *I* was ashamed.

Here's the thing. The gym, or at least a *good* gym, is supposed to be a positive space to enjoy the sweet release of endorphins. SO, to help ease the transition into the gym, please enjoy my personal 8 Queer Gym Commandments:

1. **THOU SHALT KEEP IT LOOSE**

    Both in technique and clothing. You don't need to pay top $ for those Lululemon Spanx. (Spanx? Is that what they sell?) All you need to get a good work out in is to wear something comfortable that makes YOU feel healthy, strong, hot, or a combo. (But please for the love of God do NOT wear jeans — I'm looking at you, Dominicans!) Besides, no one cares what you're wearing, because everyone is too busy worrying about other people caring about what THEY'RE wearing.

2. **THOU SHALT LIFT WEIGHTS**

    I know. Working out. It's not for everyone. But Joseph Gordon-Levitt looks like a toe, and people are into that, so anything is possible! Don't know where to start? The internet is a wonderful place with *tonssss* of workouts. Queer athlete Lori Lindsey, for example, is always posting different workout regiments on social media. And remember, just because someone is lifting more weight than you, doesn't mean you deserve to be at the gym *less* than they do. Everyone has to start somewhere. That guy making a big show scream-grunting while bench pressing 300lbs, for example? He had to start by picking up his fragile ego every single day. And look at him now.

3. **THOU SHALT BRING (OR MAKE) A BUDDY**
   It can be overwhelming going to the gym alone, so bringing a buddy can help alleviate anxieties and help you laugh through the pain. You can even watch *Law & Order* together as you get your power walking on. Don't have a buddy? Start by befriending the front desk. Ask them if they've ever seen *Law & Order: Special Victims Unit*. Then, work your way up to a convo with someone at the water fountain. If all else fails, just start talking to yourself in the crowded locker room about how *Law & Order: Trial By Jury* deserves a second season. Someone is BOUND to jump into that convo. And if they don't, you don't want those people as friends anyway.

4. **THOU SHALT NOT CHAFE**
   Girl. Chafing is NO joke, so be careful. Make sure you put powder on your hands or work out with gloves. If you're running, deodorant in between both thighs, and keep those nipples safe with a

sports bra or tank. If your nipples are pierced, keep them covered. Also, does that hurt, and should I get mine done?

5. THOU SHALT FIGHT THE FUNK

The gym *is* dirty. Not AS dirty as your thoughts of Janelle Monáe and Tessa Lynne Thompson together, but still, my God, it's filthy. So please, please, PLEASE, even though you may feel awkward in the space, shower after your workout. Or, at the very least, wash your arms and hands before putting on other clothing. Also, spare underwear, socks, and bras go a loooong way.

6. THOU SHALT NOT SELFIE

I understand you're "working" for that "bod," but please no gym selfies.

7. THOU SHALT SAUNA

After a long workout, you've earned a good schvitz in the sauna. You might be wondering: Is it okay to have sex in there? Look, it's okay not to have sex in the sauna. But also, it's *very* okay to have sex in the sauna. It's basically designed for people to have sex in there! It's hot, which means the less clothing the better. It is *literally* a place to let off steam. And if you're getting sweaty, that means you're doing it right.

8. THOU SHALT HAVE FUN

Most importantly, the gym is the temple of the body AND the mind. More often than not, your greatest enemy is you. At some point, I realized it wasn't the cis hets that were making me uncomfortable at the gym. It was me. So, the only way for me to enjoy the gym was to laugh more and focus less on how I was perceived. Yes, you're there to work out, but have fun and be yourself. That's all anyone will remember you for anyway, so make the most of it. Even if it means not wearing jeans to the gym. ENOUGH already!

NATURE

Originally, the Pride flag had a pink stripe that represented sex. While that stripe was dropped (due to a lack of available pink fabric), the green stripe, representing nature, remained. I have met so many queer people with an innate connection to the natural world. (Seriously, there are entire swaths of the internet dedicated to the gay houseplant community.)

However, what's more natural, more animalistic than sex? Maybe I'm just forever an indoor child, but, for me, that's about as natural as it gets.

These stories hold nothing back, so unclutch those pearls, unclench, and get ready to receive a sampling of the great, expansive world of queer sex.

THE WHIZ KID

by Kevin Allison

Do you remember that Zoloft commercial with the blobby little dude, shaped like an egg, and the announcer says, "Do you have SOCIAL ANXIETY?" Meanwhile, you're pouring your third glass of wine saying, "Social anxiety? Yes! I'm like that blob!" Well, that's what I was thinking for four days straight a couple years back when I finally returned to kink camp.

Now, the first time I went to one of those big outdoor sexfests was in 2011. But I always said to myself, "Kevin, if you go back, don't go alone! Bring a friend with benefits." It's best to have someone you're guaranteed to get kinky with if nothing else works out. I did meet a friend at that first kink camp I went to named Bart, but he was not my type. He was a giant ol' teddy bear with a beard down to his belly. He said, "Kev, you think this camp's nuts? Things are even more intense at kink camps just for men. They don't have as many rules about consent and, you know, decency. They just make a casual announcement at lunch, like, 'Hey guys, if someone has a heart attack, and someone prolly will, please just have the courtesy to take your dick outta your hand long enough to call for an EMT'."

Bart said one camp like that was so "underground," you can only go if someone invited you. So two summers ago, he invited me. We were getting out of the car and most of the 300 men there were already having cocktails in the sunshine. The thing was, I'd failed to convince a play-partner to accompany me this time. Ever been to a party where everyone knows everyone but you know no one? The voices in my head were saying, "What if no one likes me?" and "What's the worst that could happen?"

The day before, my therapist had asked, "Well, Kevin, when it comes to being around other men, what IS the worst that's happened?" I said, "Well, I spent my whole childhood falling in love with other boys. But, I was terrified that if one ever found out how I felt, he wouldn't just reject me, but hurt me. When I was in the 7th grade, I finally came out to my best friend Ben, whom I had a crush on. He stared at me and said, 'You're sick. You disgust me'." I'd never been so hurt.

But surely nothing like that would happen at this cocktail party at kink camp! No, but what did happen was that suddenly, a chubby guy standing right next to me started screaming bloody murder as a bunch of men carried him off, tied him to a fence, and pelted him with paintballs. I thought, "Wait … THAT might happen to me? Does this campground have a washer and dryer? I only brought one pair of jeans."

Bart said, "That's an ambush. Usually happens to newbies." I got myself a vodka. I decided right then to fall off the wagon for the weekend. Bart said, "Just try to say 'yes' … and don't yuck on someone's yum." Maybe you've heard that expression? People in kink circles say, "Don't yuck on my yum," meaning that if you meet someone who has a fetish that freaks you out, try not to say, "EWWWW!"

Keep that in mind for what comes next.

Bart showed me a form with my name on it. He said, "Everyone gets a 'dance card.' On the first day, we all schedule all kinds of kinky appointments. I'll sign you up on some dates." He came back 10 minutes later saying, "I got your first date! It's at 9:30 tomorrow morning, and it's needles!" I said, "NEEDLES?!" I wasn't entirely sure what that meant, but all I could say was, "They don't *hurt*, do they?" He said, "Oh, boy ... *they sure do*! But you're in the best hands. His name is Mister Prickly."

The next morning, in the dungeon, which was really just a big old barn, I met Mister Prickly. He looked like Santa Claus. "Oh gooooooood! I'm going to create a ginger pin cushion!" he said. I stripped, he tied me to a table, and he pinched a little bit of the skin on my chest and said, "take a deep breath in ... and now let it out," as he pushed a needle through. I lit up all over.

I thought, "YEP! It stings!" But then I breathed again and said, "Okay, but it wasn't that bad." Then that pattern repeated again and again. Finally, he said, "Now, guess how many needles are stuck in you?" I was laying down and couldn't move to get a view. I said, "60?" He said, "Goddamn! It's 59. You're really good at that!" So I have that talent, I guess ... but then he went to put the next one in me, and I found my brain tensing up yet again, thinking, "Oh, no, it's gonna hurt!" Then, it was in, and I thought, "but it's not that bad ..." And it dawned on me: I've had this same thought pattern 60 times. It was just like all the social anxiety on the trip so far. My brain says, "What if they're not nice to me? What's the worst that could happen?" But, then, real life happens, and almost always ... it's not that bad. I shared this with Mr. Prickly, and he said, "Well, now keep that little lesson in mind if you end up being ambushed this weekend."

Two days later, I was back in that dungeon late at night and I was mesmerized. I was watching two twinky lads; smooth, skinny young fellas, just my type and completely naked. They hovered 10 feet in the air because a rope-tying master had made them into marionettes. He pulled the ropes so that one would end up with his face in the other's crotch one moment, then an ass in the face the next. I thought, "So much of the kink scene is like going on rides at an amusement park."

A crowd of us stared in wonder at this puppet show when, suddenly, I became aware that a young man I'd been flirting with all weekend was standing next to me — a Puerto Rican guy named Diego. He was in his 20s with curly hair and a constant mischievous grin. Next to him was an older guy I didn't know, a real rugged looking guy, might as well have been an army commander. We can call him Ed Harris. Anyway, Diego said, "I might have to take a date off my dance card so I can attend the water sports party tomorrow." And Ed Harris said, "Don't dress up!" I said, "Yeah, I'm curious about that. Ya know, I couldn't believe how turned on I was the first time a guy used me as a urinal."

Now, this might be a good place to pause the story. Especially if you're currently yucking on my yum.

I wasn't lying. About a year earlier, a fella named Cheng that I sometimes played with, surprised me. He put me on my knees in the shower, told me to open my mouth, and let loose a torrent of pee that seemed to go on forever. I worshipped Cheng. When he got all dominant like that, he made me swoon. He looked like a Chinese Harry Potter, was alarmingly well-endowed, and was full of surprises. There's something especially worshipful about being on your knees and relishing even a person's nastiest stuff. As long as he's not one of those guys whose pee tastes like a rotten lime soaked in battery acid.

Back to kink camp.

You'll recall that Diego and Ed were standing there talking to me when I said, "Ya know, I couldn't believe how turned on I was the first time a guy used me as a urinal." Well. Diego looked at Ed. Ed looked at Diego. They nodded. And the ambush began.

Ed grabbed me in a headlock. Diego pushed me out of the dungeon. Ed yelled, "We have a urinal here!" I was saying, "Oh no no no no!" but anyone could see, my body was not resisting. Diego got handcuffs on my wrists behind my back and you know what I felt when they clicked? Relief. A weekend of worrying about the worst that could happen, but now that might be it, I let go. The click of the cuffs, becoming the center of attention, and being dominated by two hot guys I instinctively trusted — everything was shifting. I wasn't a guy worrying over possibilities in his head. In the entrapment, I didn't have options for second guessing where I was going — and that was freeing. I was going with the flow … in more ways than one.

They brought me outside to a grassy knoll, and there was a line to use the bathroom outside the barn. Ed shouted to the shadows, "Don't use those urinals! Use THIS one!" Diego said to someone, "Take his cell phone out of his pocket." Someone took my phone and threw it where it wouldn't get wet, unlike my shirt and jeans. I thought, "Christ. I still don't know if there's a washer and dryer anywhere on these campgrounds." But I felt taken care of because of the phone, like on some level, Diego and Ed were being respectful to me.

They shoved me to my knees, as shadowy figures started hovering all above. Diego went first. That mischievous grin had some sweetness shining through it, and his skin was soft and warm. He pulled out his cock, and as the water flowed, men shouted, "Open your mouth!" which I did with pleasure. I put my lips around his cock and sucked for his piss like a thirsting man at an oasis. His piss was refreshing. With Diego, I was in bliss.

Now in kink circles, you'll sometimes hear men say, "A urinal should have no opinion about the piss. His job is just to take it." Well, I had opinions. Ed Harris was up next and the taste was harsher, but he was also pissing like a racehorse. He could tell that he was practically waterboarding me, so he pulled back and shot it all over the crown of my head, in my eyes, on my chest. It was a baptism. I moaned half in desire, half in dread. I could hardly see with so much piss dripping in my eyes, but I arched my back to lean toward them all to take more. That's when a bunch of them let loose, maybe six streams coming at me at once. A river running down my chest into a pool at the crotch of my jeans.

Then there was a weird moment when a man about 80 years old was shuffled to the front of the crowd. Someone yelled, "Suck his cock, too," and I found myself playing along, with my mouth on this elderly nub of a dick, pretending it was *not* not my thing. I'm thrilled that gerontophiles exist — guys who have the hots for our elders. I'll be even more thrilled for their existence when *I'm* 80. But there was no time to think about that, because by then a big muscle jock was shoving at me saying, "Open that mouth again, faggot." I couldn't see him through the piss in my eyes, but I didn't like his tone. He sounded like a bully. I know it sounds nuts, but he sounded like he was going to piss in my mouth without showing me respect.

So, you see, what feels consensual can shift in a split second. Nevertheless, like in improv, I "committed to the bit." I opened my mouth, and an explosion of the foulest piss I've ever tasted hit the back of my throat. Without thinking, I barfed it all right back up all over his jeans! His pants were soaked. He screamed, "What the fuck?!" He was still pissing, and I was still coughing it back onto him. He said, "Fuck! This faggot got piss all over me!!!" And Ed Harris patted his chest and pushed him away saying, "Okay, alright, that's enough then."

The last streams died down, and I had one last little drink from beautiful Diego to wash away the nastiness. I was a hot, wet mess on my knees in the grass as guys zipped up their flies and said, "Goddamn, was that hot. That guy's quite a piss pig." Diego unclicked the cuffs and whispered, "You were amazing. Let me get you your phone." Ed Harris helped me up saying, "Look at you! You are steaming in the cool night air!"

I was proud. I had let go of worrying for a while, and got to experience the good, the bad, and the ugly. That muscle jock … HE was the worst thing that happened that weekend. I cannot respect a man who shows no respect. It turns out, even handcuffed, in an ambush, I would not submit to him. As I walked away, Ed leaned into me and whispered, "Thanks for playing, Bud. You gave that one guy what he deserved. I hope you're starting to feel at home here."

As I sloshed back to my cabin in the night, a tall, thin, sweet looking stranger emerged from the shadows, wearing a long, blonde wig and a tutu. "Hello, dear," he said. "Oh. Don't touch me," I said. "I'm sopping wet! I just got pissed on." He said, "Oh, I *know* you did, darling. That's why I'm here! I'm Andy, the guardian angel of water sports at camp.

And after a fella falls into a sticky situation like you did just now, I like to share a special gift with him."

I stared at this amazing figure in wonder. I said, "What gift is that?"

He held out a shiny object in his hand and said, "The key to the secret laundry room."

A BRIEF STORY ABOUT LOSING MY VIRGINITY (TO A DUDE. CAN YOU IMAGINE? THE VERY IDEA!)

by Drae Campbell

When I was about [mutter, mutter]-years-old, I was in college. It was the early '90s, and there was this guy I had a crush on. His name was Jay, and I just thought he was really neat and cool and fabulous. He was kind of flowy and tall, and he was a Gemini and bisexual.

Having a crush on a bisexual guy in the '90s isn't really anything of note, but ME having a crush on a flowy, tall, bisexual Gemini might come as a surprise to folks who know me now. Today, I'm a white, 40-something, genderqueer, butch lesbian. I have very short, close-cropped, salt-and-pepper hair. My gender presentation is rather masculine, and I'm often mistaken for a man ... which I don't mind.

Back then, I was kind of bisexual-ish myself. I had rosy cheeks and long, blonde, curly hair. I wore ripped Levi's and half shirts, and I wrote long, Anne Lister-type letters to a gal I had a deep crush on. I'd had yet to make out with a woman, but I dated and made out with men with more ease and probably a little less focus. We didn't really use the word "queer" the way we do now. As a matter of fact, "queer" was still probably considered a bit of a slur at that time, yet to be reclaimed. I think of queer in so many ways. To me, queer has become a movement that has radically expanded and challenged the idea of who you are in your body, in your desire, in your gender, and so much more. We had fewer words to ID ourselves with, and, to be honest, there was still the sting of shame and secrecy lingering from generations past.

Being socialized as a straight, cis woman, fed me into the idea that 'losing my virginity' meant having penetrative sex with a cis man. That's just how I understood 'losing my virginity,' despite coming from a relatively queer-friendly working class family. (We now know virginity is a bullshit construct, just like gender, which makes this story feel even more quaint.)

I had 'hooked up' with and crushed out on lots of guys in the past, just hadn't had actual intercourse, so to speak. Somewhere along the line, I decided I was going to lose my virginity to Jay. During the course of our friendship, he had told me lots of wild, wonderful stories from his life. He was so young, I often wondered if they were true. I'm sure that was part of the allure for me. He had a tendency to be a bit duplicitous and difficult to pin down, but he was also dedicated to me and seemed convinced of my talents as an actor — a classic Gemini.

We were in a very intense theater program together. Jay grew up in a small town in the Pacific Northwest. One of the many stories he told me was that he had done sex work in this small town where he grew up. He told me that he would sleep with his friends' mothers for money. He was essentially a prostitute. That's one of the things we called 'sex work' at that time. Prostitution, hustling, what have you.

Looking back, I wonder if I was thinking "maybe you're gonna do a little sex work *for me.*" We seemed to be attracted to each other and spent a lot of time together, so I decided to ask if he would be willing to deflower me. After some consideration, he agreed.

"I'll devirginize you, but you're probably gonna be like 'What's the big deal'?"

Not a lot of confidence there. Or maybe too much?

The day we decided to do the deed, we went to my dorm room. My college campus was on a former army barracks, so our dorms were very basic. The walls were particle board, the land adjacent to our campus boasted the danger of live mines, rattlesnakes, and explosive eucalyptus trees, as noted on a 'warning' letter in all the dorms. Our dorms were built on stilts on the side of a rocky hill, and we could hear everything through the walls.

I shared a bedroom, and I slept on the top bunk. My roommate was out, but Jay and I still had to get on the shaky top bunk. I insisted on playing a tape while we did it. Not just any tape, but Bette Midler's comedy album "Mud Will Be Flung Tonight."

This strange detail really speaks to me as I reflect on the history of my sexuality and my gender. I feel so seen by my younger self. Hearing Bette tell jokes and sing cabaret songs in the background of my first real bone was probably some sort of comforting way to grasp reality as my body entered the world of SEX. (*We had a condom and everything!*) And we proceeded to lose my virginity, together.

Jay was right. I was kind of like, was that it? It was painful and strange and not as totally magical as I had half hoped.

A few months later, there was a blood drive being done by the Red Cross at my school campus. I decided to do a good deed and donate some blood. (Also, I heard there would be cookies.) The people collecting the blood and facilitating the donations were local, little old lady volunteers. To determine if you were suited to donate blood at that time, you were given a list of about 100 or so "yes or no" questions to answer on a piece of paper. If you answered "yes" to any of the questions, you were not allowed to donate blood. Those were local ladies donating their time, and I was a fresh-faced, 'straight-looking' young woman.

I answered all the questions thoughtfully and handed them the paper. The group of volunteers stared at the paper across the room, eyeing me suspiciously. Looking back and forth, back and forth. I smiled, but I also became a little nervous at their hesitation. They appeared to be painfully deciding who had to break the news to me. Finally, one lady with tightly curled, white hair ambled over. She seemed a little embarrassed.

"We can't let you give blood, dear."

It was my one "yes" answer on the long list of blood donor questions. The question was: "Have you ever had sex with a prostitute?" My answer was indeed "yes." I had sex, as I understood it, exactly one time in my life, and it was with a person who had, at one point, identified as a male prostitute. Was he lying? I had to take his word and report the facts as I knew them. There was no space for nuance in those "yes or no" questions. Why would Jay make that up anyway? I had to fess up. We were talking about blood here. After she told me I was rejected, I became ashamed ... but also a little proud to have been THAT WEIRDO to them. I thought of those suburbanites imagining the story they thought was attached to my single "yes" and have it forever challenge their assumptions.

The elderly do-gooder who had to break the news seemed to want to find out everything about what she thought my little world was. I could only imagine the questions she had burning in her mind? Who was this prostitute? Did I need help? Are you a prostitute? Part of me wanted to contextualize my "yes" and explain to this grandmotherly group, but would they get it? For all I knew, maybe they were former sex workers who retired in a San Diego suburb. Who was making assumptions now?

No, they were there simply to take blood. That's all. Like some Pollyanna judgmental vampires. I walked out in shame (and without cookies). Sex complicates everything.

(On a side note, it's worth pointing out that to this day, gay men are still not allowed to give blood if they've had sex in the last year. Get it together, RED CROSS!)

Maybe I was ahead of my time. Jay certainly was. I had just had my first penetrative, heterosexual, cisgender, ol' fashioned, straight sex but, in the eyes of those elders, I was still the gal who fucked a hooker and wanted to give blood. Even at the very 'straightest' I could be, I managed to queer the simple act of giving blood … and the not-so-simple act of losing my virginity.

THE HORSE FAIR

by Philip Markle

"Red blindfold or white blindfold?" asked the bouncer wearing assless chaps and a T-shirt with a logo of a horse's ass above the name 'Fickstutenmark.' "Red means bareback is OK. White means condom only." That was the second thing asked of me at The Horse Fair — the kinkiest, craziest, sexiest, scariest thing I have ever done in my life. The first question the bouncer asked me was, "Have you read the FAQ?"

Daniel Nardicio, the notorious gay nightclub promoter and self-titled King of Sleaze, had told me about The Horse Fair when I mentioned I was going to Berlin. "It's this insane party. You choose whether you will be a stallion or a mare," he said in-between doing five other things at once. "If you're a stallion, you walk around and fuck any mare you want. If you're a mare, they put a blindfold on you and tie you up somewhere in the stable, and you're fucked for hours by anonymous D. It's a great time!"

A week later, I was in Berlin and enjoying some afternoon biers with my lady friends from NYC when I off-handedly mentioned The Horse Fair. Like, in a "Isn't this insane?! Isn't Berlin so crazy! Isn't this wretched madness?" sort of way. What I didn't expect was for the ladies to all start pounding the wooden table and chanting: "Pumped full of cum! Pumped full of cum!"

As good (or bad) luck would have it, The Horse Fair was happening the very next day in the basement of The KitKatClub at 5 p.m. The ladies insisted I must go. I had to experience it. Even if I wasn't sure I wanted to go, they reminded me to think of the content. The song I could write. The Medium.com article I could compose. The need for #Content demanded that I become a horse for a day.

I gulped down my bier and told my friends I would think about it. It's no secret I'm a horny bottom. I've only topped a man once in my life, and it was during the witching hour of New Year's Eve last year when I woke between 2–3 a.m., and, in a haze, begun to fuck my one-night stand. It was like a sexual demon possessed me for five minutes, and while somewhat pleasurable, it was not my preferred *modus operandi*, and I didn't stay hard long. The demon abated, and I was left wanting only to be fucked in return. Other than that single encounter, my best chance of topping a guy at this point is probably after I'm dead via *rigor mortis*.

I love to bottom. I love to be fucked by a great top. But, while I've fantasized about BDSM play or watched my share of "hardcore" pornos, I've never actually been tied up or done any sort of submissive/dominant role-playing. At best, I've been rough handled a bit during sex — spanked, lightly choked, forced to listen to a Tenacious D album — all of which is still pretty vanilla in the wide world of gay sex. At longest, I'd been fucked for about an hour. How was this basic bottom bitch going to survive a parade of stallions doing whatever they wanted with me for six?!

I couldn't sleep the night before The Fair. I turned on my roaming cellular data and burned megabytes downloading extreme pornos on my iPhone to see if they put me in the mood. Sure enough, I felt my body primed with electricity, a current of *antici … pation* running through me — nervous, but also excited, for a new test. Like how I felt the day before I took my high school SATs. The idea of not having any control or say in what happened felt antithetical to how any sexual attraction should work. I liked looking at a guy across a bar and scoping the chemistry. This would just be me checking out the inside of a cloth bag. But there was magic in this powerlessness, in the anonymity, in losing my personhood to become equine.

I switched from watching porn to pouring over The Horse Fair's FAQ:

- Once I chose my preference, I could not switch roles. (I would go as a mare. There was little chance of me enjoying being a stallion. #MareForever.)
- I would be blindfolded with a cloth bag over my head — covering everything except my nose and mouth (for breathing and other uses).
- I would be buck-ass naked except for shoes and tube socks (recommended for storing poppers).
- All the mares would arrive first at 5 p.m. to undress, enjoy a bier, and socialize. Then, at 6:30 p.m., we would be tied up somewhere in "the stable." The stallions would arrive and inspect that day's selection of meat — examine us, compare our physical attributes, and decide which mare each wanted to break-in.
- Then, mares would be at the mercy of the stallions, passed around horse to horse, for the next six hours!

- But I could leave whenever I wanted if I was uncomfortable. I could get help by raising my hands above my head, and a staff member not participating in the fuckfest would come to the rescue: be it toilet, bier, water, cigarette, or just a chance to go into the mare's changing room and give this horse a rest.
- I had the right to ensure whomever was fucking me was wearing a condom. Safe sex was strictly enforced if you chose the white bag. And, I could refuse a stallion on the condition he was condom-less or — as the website put it — "too well-hung." This had to be the only sex party in the world where too big a dick was grounds for rejection.

There was a parade of mares in line when I arrived at The KitKatClub at 5 p.m. the next day. No one was making eye contact with one another, despite the fact we were all consenting to this insane adventure. I asked to bum a cigarette from a cute guy named Erich behind me in line. I asked if he'd ever done something like this. No, he was a horse virgin like me. We giggled and chatted about how the weather was quite hot, then — silence.

I took out my phone and texted my female friends who had motivated me to do this, my two final thoughts:

First: "Well, I'm off to the races!"

Followed by: "As Mary Poppins says, 'If we must, we must!'"

My last thought before I descended into the curated slice of Hell was Mary Poppins agreeing to join a tea party on the ceiling. She loved to laugh; I loved to neigh.

We entered and each paid the 12 Euro admission fee. We went downstairs into the Dragon Room of the KitKat-

Club. Ultraviolet light painted a picture of a two-story sex dungeon, replete with everything you'd find in any darkroom — from the forest of glory holes to den of slings slung from every orifice. I met the bouncer who made sure I was properly informed of the FAQ. He asked if I wanted to take a Polaroid to compete for the "Ass Of The Month." I passed.

I went to the Mare's changing room, took off all my clothes and put them in the provided extra-large trash bag. The bag check man wrote a number on my arm in blue Sharpie — branding me Mare #50. I ran into Erich again at the bar. I began chain-smoking Vogue cigarettes and downing gin & tonics, ordered via the number on my arm (to be paid for when I left). The bartender noticed I was nervous and gave me a hard time about it in the way that shows a gay really cares. He sassed me right out of my doubts, and by 6:30 p.m., I was grinning and drunk.

"It's time," said the bouncer. "The stallions are waiting."

"Giddy up!" I said and raised my glass to no one. I drained it and realized just how late I was to be tied up in the stable. Every spot in the crowded two-floor dungeon was taken up with a bound and blindfolded mare. I walked over with my white bag and asked where I should go. "Sling?" asked the staff member, pointing to the only free spot in the vicinity. "Sure, sounds fun," I said, without a thought. They secured the blindfold over my head and helped helpless me into the sling, binding both my feet in the air.

I found myself rock hard waiting for the market to open. They were pumping remixed disco Donna Summer throughout the Horse Market. "I Feel Love" reverberated in my mind and my body. There is no greater feeling in the world than waiting for something new to begin.

I heard the sounds of the stallions entering; I felt air move beneath my ankles as they passed me. After about two minutes, a stallion sidled up to me and touched my leg. I gasped in surprise. He began caressing me, moving up the length of my body until he met my lips. He offered me poppers, and I inhaled as deeply as I could. He was gentle and took things slow. He entered me, built up the pace, and we had glorious sex for about 15 minutes. I loved every minute of it.

He gave me a kiss goodbye and left me there, glistening in sweat and euphoria. But almost immediately, I felt someone else plow their way into me. And then, my girlfriends' prescient theme song "Pumped Full Of Cum" came into fruition.

There was a line of men at the sling waiting to fuck me. I had made a rookie mistake. I thought the sling would be a relaxing place to pass the time in repose. Little did I know, the sling was an advanced choice. The sling was the parking garage for the event, and, one by one, men came and parked themselves inside me.

There was no break. I tried to relax and roll with the insanity, find a way to be turned on by the onslaught, but it was relentless. I could only identify different men by the varying size and girth of their members. It was like speed dating by dick. The sweat from twelve different men on my body was a kind of primal-smelling funk. I began to panic; I felt overwhelmed; and I needed a break. I raised my hand and right away an attendance came to my aid. "What do you want?" he asked. "Break! Beer! Toilet! Whatever!" I said, glad my voice hadn't transformed into that of a horse. Something human remained.

The attendant led blindfolded me into the break room and took the mask off. My right leg wouldn't stop shaking. I was in shock — the fantasy turned near nightmare by sheer intensity. I thought about leaving — but I hadn't cum yet, and lord knows I believe in capitalism; I wasn't going to take that much and not get my rocks off before I left.

I sat down and drank my bier until my body calmed itself. I saw other men in there also taking a break; I wasn't the only one who'd called a time-out just 30 minutes into the event. I gathered my wits about me, put the blindfold back on and asked to be led back into the breach.

This time, I found myself deposited in a corner where the rate of men approaching me to play was at a more leisurely pace. Some even talked to me: asked me where I was from, told me how handsome I was, teased by asking what I wanted done to me. One guy, in-between kisses, told me about his recent trip to South Africa. He suggested some sites I should visit one day. I just said, "Danke."

Then, the Prize Horse came up to me. I couldn't describe what he looked like, but I felt his face, and the aspect ratio of his eyes, nose, cheek bones, and lips seemed to conform to the Golden Ratio! He must have been attractive. I decided that his face was that of my favorite porn star, because why not? He could be anyone I wanted him to be. My fingers explored his body — his chiseled chest, strong back, taut stomach — he was an Adonis from stern to bow. I played with his hair — how nice, the simple discovery that he had luscious, thick locks that fell to his shoulders. It reminded me of Western paintings of our Lord and Savior Jesus Christ. And like Christ, he had a heavenly dick. We took things slow. We kept at it, in union with one another — the stallion and the mare — for at least 30 minutes. I experienced a full body orgasm, and the ecstasy was incredible. He finished at the same time as me, thanked me, kissed my ear, and left me alone.

I raised my hand and said, "Done, thanks! Check please!"

The bouncers teased me as I dressed. "What?! Only two hours!" they said. "You have four more to go!"

"I'm good," I replied, smirking. I had done it, done something that the Philip 24 hours before wouldn't have dared if not for the push over the ledge from his friends who know best.

I paid my tab at the bar and left The Horse Fair, but not without first peeking into the main room. Like Orpheus leaving Hell, I couldn't resist one last look. And I saw with my eyes everything that had been a fantasy before. It was a grotesque picture of men fucking bagged men every which way like animals. The visual disturbed me and tainted the movie in my mind, which had been so much sexier than reality. My last thought as I climbed the stairway into the afternoon sunset was, "I wish I hadn't looked."

I wonder if some people may find this story frightening or even problematic, given the fuzzy boundaries around consent at this shindig. The truth was, I knew what I had signed up for and bought into the rules. I felt immense kindness from the staff; I felt taken care of and that they truly wanted me to enjoy myself. I would estimate I had sex with 16 strangers. I rode the wave of the experience, be it extricating myself when it was overwhelming, to surrendering to the kink to have one of the best orgasms of my life. It was — all in all — a sex-positive adventure.

I don't know if this mare will ever go back to the stables. One day at the races may have been enough. That said, the name Philip translates to "lover of horses" in Ancient Greek, so never say never.

HARMONY

No, I'm not referring to the angelic intonations of The Supremes or ABBA or Destiny's Child. The most gorgeous harmonies aren't reserved for only the musically inclined.

The same principle still applies: people combine their talents to create something beautiful. There's an exchange of energy, each person's part positioned perfectly in relation to the other. When it happens sonically, it has the power to move you to tears; when it happens on an emotional level, it has the power to change lives.

Relationships are the pursuit of that harmony. And, like some of the following stories, the results are not always beautiful music. But, for every moment of discord, there are incredible, passionate performances of a song we sing to each other over cocktails, on long drives, in tangles of bedsheets, and in our most private moments.

IMPOSSIBLE LITTLE JIMMY

by Jamie Brickhouse

Back in the last century, I was strolling down Columbus Avenue on New York's Upper West Side one balmy, yummy Saturday afternoon. It was the first hot day of summer, and the streets were pulsing with people wearing as little as legally possible. I had nothing on my agenda but sex with a perfect stranger. But where to find him? This was before Grindr and Scruff took over. The apps are supposed to tell you exactly what you're getting before you get it. You know, labels like "top," "bottom," "vers," — *yeah, right* — "water sports," "nip play," etcetera, etcetera, *etcetera*. In the old days, you figured out that stuff as you went along and did the work on the ground. That was part of the adventure. I'm a proud descendant of hunters and gatherers.

It was a perfect day to forage in The Ramble, the bosky part of Central Park dotted with bird watchers and one-eyed snake seekers, a gay Bob Ross painting. First, I decided to play my other favorite sport, daytime drinking, and I hit my neighborhood gay bar, The Works.

I walked into the bar from the glare of the sunny day into the gloaming of that dark cave. The cool hum of the air conditioning caressed my body. As my eyes became adjusted to the gloom, I discovered there were several tasty possibilities, but I chose to sit at the bar next to an impossibility, i.e. a super-hot guy out of my league. He looked like a pint-sized George Clooney, *E.R.*-TV-show-Clooney. It wasn't his Clooney charisma that magnetized me to the metal bar stool next to him. He looked like Chris. Chris from college. Everybody wanted to sleep with Chris, and Chris slept with just about everybody. Except me. We were good friends. Four years out of college, and I was still mad that I never had him, even when I once had the chance.

A lanky, copper-redhead, I'm a cutie pie, the funny sidekick. Sometimes sexy, but never hot. Still, I've never gone hungry. I can close the deal most of the time because of my boldness, willingness, enthusiasm. I'm like a cabaret performer who can't really sing, but can sell a song through sheer personality.

I ordered my drink: martini, Beefeater gin, up, dry, with a twist. I sideways glanced at Impossible, who sat on his stool elbow-bending a Rolling Rock beer. He was dressed like Chris would — navy-blue Izod and khaki shorts — his olive complexion just starting to tan. I was wearing shorts, too. I shifted my focus and discovered that my martini had made its entrance. *How long was that glance?* I took a long, deep sip, flashing my male gaze at him. He mirrored me and pulled on the neck of his Rolling Rock and took a swig. I led.

"Hey, I'm Jamie," I said.

"Hey, Jamie." Impossible introduced himself. "What are you up to?"

"Oh, nothing much. Looking for some fun."

"What kind of fun?" Impossible said with a sly grin.

"Sex." I told you I'm bold.

He said, "Oh, yeah? What are you into?"

"Oh, I don't know. I just like sex." I gave my martini a rim job — circling the edge of the glass with my index finger. His bare knee pressed into my bare leg.

"You know, I live just two blocks from here," I said.

"Just two blocks, huh?" Impossible flashed that same sly grin.

"Yep."

Convenience is a crucial factor in sealing the deal. If the competition standing next to you is hotter than you, but you live two blocks away and he lives in another neighborhood, you're going to win.

"So, do you have any fantasies that turn you on?" Impossible asked.

"Not really," I said "I just like sex and going where the moment takes us."

"Oh, come on, what's your wildest fantasy?"

I've never been into kink. It's not something I seek; however, I'm a people pleaser, compliant. If you want me to fist fuck you, I'll fist fuck you. I've done it a few times. The first time was in college. I picked up a guy in a bar and we ended up in the back seat of my car. He asked me to stick a couple of fingers up his ass. Two fingers became three. Three became four. Four became . . . *Look, Ma, no hand!* I almost lost my high school class ring. I made the mistake of revealing this to my friends during a game of Truth or Dare. It earned me the unshakeable moniker "Puppet Man."

And if you want me to pee on you, I'll pee on you. Just don't pee on me. I'll even can my piss, if that's what you want. On my way out of Blow Buddies, a sex club in San Francisco, I hurriedly gave the clothes check guy my claim check. "Here you go," I said. He was drinking an O'Doul's beer. "I'll be right back. I've gotta pee really bad."

A smile crept over his face. "Really bad?"

"Yep. Pretty bad," I said.

He chugged the rest of the O'Doul's and handed me the empty can.

"Do me a favor, Buddy, pee into this."

So I did. And he drank it. I told you I'm a people pleaser.

And if you want me to be a wayward, runaway, teenage boy to your Father Ritter of Boys Town, I'm your guy. That was a game my common-law husband Michael and I used to play early in our relationship. Don't get icked out by the whole priest-teenage boy thing. The whole point of role play is to do something that's forbidden or even illegal in the real world. We usually played it while taking a bath together. He'd say, "Hey, kid, it must feel good to have a nice hot bath after hitch-hiking those highways all that time."

I'd answer in my best gee-whiz-teen-hustler voice, "Yeah, Father, it sure does. It feels real good. And that. Feels. Real. Good. Too." Then we'd get out of the bathtub and have our own hot sex.

I draw the line at scat. I leave that to Ella Fitzgerald.

I said to Impossible at The Works: "Well, you asked the question, so I'll bet you have a fantasy in mind."

"Yeah, I do," he said.

"All right, come on. Give it up."

"Well, growing up, my best friend was Jimmy. Little Jimmy. His daddy was Big Jimmy, so everybody called him Little Jimmy. We lived on the same block. We were so close, we'd just walk into each other's rooms and never knock. I always had a crush on him. I don't know if Little Jimmy even knew it or maybe felt the same way. So, anyway, when I was in junior high, one afternoon I went over to his house, and I walked in through the back kitchen door like I always did. I said 'hello' to Little Jimmy's mom. I asked her if Little Jimmy was home. 'Yeah, he's upstairs in his room.' I said, 'Thanks, I'll go on up.' So, I went upstairs …"

"Yeah?"

"And his door was shut, but it was slightly cracked open …"

"Uh-huh …"

"And I pushed open the door …"

"I'm with you," I said.

"And there was Little Jimmy …"

"What was he doing?"

As Impossible told me this, he didn't look at me, but just past me, his eyes glazed over in a Little Jimmy reverie. It turned me on watching him get turned on by this old childhood memory. Even though he wasn't looking at me, he was pressing that bare knee harder into my bare leg.

I was rapt. "Go on," I said. Impossible was a very good storyteller.

"So, there was Little Jimmy, and he was on the bed. His bare butt was in the air, and his Fruit of the Loom tightie whities were tangled up around his ankles, and he was humping his pillow."

"That's hot."

"So, I stood there for a couple of seconds and then I said …" Impossible paused, gulped, and spoke in a stage whisper of reverence and awe: "'Little Jimmy.'"

After a beat, Impossible continued the story.

"Little Jimmy slowly looked over his left shoulder at me. He was beet red. He said, 'Hey, buddy.'" There was a catch and quiver in Impossible's Little Jimmy voice, "'You … you caught me.' And I said, 'Yeah, I did, Little Jimmy.'"

"Then what'd you do?"

"I walked up to the front of the bed, and I was pretty hard …"

I mimicked his Little Jimmy catch-and-quiver voice and said, "Yeah, I'm pretty hard right now, too."

"And I got on top of the bed on my knees, and Little Jimmy reached over to my groin …"

"That's pretty hot. So, do you want to replay that little story?"

"Yeah, man. Are you up for it?" Impossible said this with the wide-eyed grin of a kid asking, "Can we really have ice cream for dinner?"

"I sure am. Now let me guess. I'm Little Jimmy, right?"

"Yep."

"All right. Give me a five-minute head start. I'll run back to my apartment."

Show time! And I did a lot of theater in college. "By the way, you're in luck. I live in a duplex, so my bedroom is a flight up. So you're going to get to walk up the stairs to the bedroom just like you did in real life." I was excited for him. "It's going to be that much more real and authentic!"

I gave him my address and gulped down the rest of my martini. I sprinted those two blocks faster than Jesse Owens. I lived in a five-floor walk up, and I took those stairs two at a time. I felt like I could lift a car and save a trapped baby so pumped was I on the adrenaline of anticipation. I got into my apartment and I raced up the stairs to my bedroom. I unmade the bed. I put the humping pillow in place. I went back downstairs, and I waited by the buzzer.

While I waited, I anticipated how we were going to play out the whole Little Jimmy thing and what his cock must be like. It dawned on me. I was finally going to get to have sex with College Chris through his doppelgänger.

There was one afternoon when College Chris and I almost did it. We were freshmen and flush in the bloom of just-out-of-the-closet friends. We were studying for a sex and ethics course. He was sitting at my desk. I was up on the top bunk bed. We veered off our study course onto a tangent about our first times. We hit a lull in the conversation. Our eyes locked. Possessed, our lips spread into smiles of desire. All I had to do was jump from the bunk. Idiot that I am, I broke the moment and said, "I don't think we ought to. We're too good of friends." That was back in the days when I still had scruples. I've regretted not going for what I wanted ever since. He wasn't the man that got away, but the lay that got away.

I continued to wait by my door buzzer for Impossible. I waited. And waited. *And waited. He's not coming,* I thought. *He just played me for a fool.* Or worse, a hotter guy who lives a block closer saddled up next to him after I left.

The squawking blare that is my apartment buzzer jolted me out of my nightmare fantasy. *Thank God.*

I buzzed him in without saying anything into the speaker and left the door unlocked. I ran upstairs and hopped on the bed. I stripped down to my tightie whities (Calvin Klein, not Fruit of the Loom, I'll have you know) and tangled them real good around my ankles, just like I'd been directed. I started humping the pillow, but I never really was a pillow humper, so I cheated a little and flipped over on my back and got myself excited with my trusted right hand. I heard him open the door downstairs so I flipped over and got back to humping the pillow. My head was going in and out almost touching the wrought iron headboard of the antique bed. I heard the door close. I heard him say 'hello' to Little Jimmy's mom. I heard him ask if Little Jimmy was at home. I heard him say,

"Thanks, I'll go on up." He said that louder than his previous words to Little Jimmy's mom, I suppose to make sure I'd heard him and would know to be ready. I cocked my head to the side as it continued to dart toward the headboard, and I thought, *Wow! He knows this story verbatim, and he's playing it down to the last inch.*

I heard him come up the stairs. Slowly. One. Step. At a time. With each step, I got harder. I heard him at the top of the stairs. I heard him push open the door. I was still pillow humping just like I'd been told to do. After a couple of seconds, I heard, "Little Jimmy." He said it in the same hushed wonder and awe as when he told me the story.

I looked over my shoulder almost in slow motion. I know my face was beet red — not from embarrassment, but from that martini, and racing those two blocks and running up those five flights of stairs. I looked at him and I said with that Little Jimmy catch-and-quiver voice, "Hey, buddy. You caught me."

He said, "Yeah, I did."

He walked up to the bed with his tenting crotch. He climbed onto the bed. He stood on his knees. I reached over. I started to unbutton his shorts. He pulled back slightly. I grabbed harder and unbuttoned his shorts and pulled them down. There were his tightie (very) whities. I pushed down the elastic for the reveal: Fruit of the Loom. It was better than I dreamed: a thick, fat, kielbasa. *Hold the bun, mustard on the side.* I head-lunged toward it. He stood up off the bed. He pulled up his underpants and shorts.

But, but?

He stuffed that beautiful kielbasa that was quickly becoming a Vienna sausage into his forbidden Fruit of the Looms. He zipped up his shorts.

With my head hanging over the side of the bed, I said, "Hey, what are you doing?"

"Thanks, buddy. That was great."

"But wait. Aren't we going to make our *own* fantasy now?"

"No, that's it."

That's it! That's it?! I didn't say that because I was in shock.

"You did a good job," Impossible said.

Thanks. You can leave the money on the dresser. I didn't say that either.

He left. I was abandoned lying on the bed draped over the pillow like a deflated condom we never got to use. Was it then that I realized when you're a people pleaser, you often don't get pleased? I heard him go down the stairs. I heard him open the door. I heard him close the door. I didn't hear him say good-bye to Little Jimmy's mom, which I thought was rude.

I thought he was a good storyteller, but me thinks this is the only story he knows. Clearly, he was in a rut! I had been patting myself on the back for perhaps being hotter than I thought because I landed this guy. But it didn't matter if I looked like Brad Pitt or Steve Buscemi. Did I even resemble Little Jimmy? It only mattered that I was willing to play the game, act out his fantasy. How many other Little Jimmy victims like me are out there? I want to find them and start a support group.

I'm on the apps these days. It's the only way to get laid, and it's easier to negotiate what you want up front. Since I don't drink anymore, the idea of hanging out at a bar and nursing an O'Doul's is not appealing for *many* reasons. The apps obliterated my old hunting grounds. There aren't any homosexuals left in The Ramble, just birds and the homo sapiens who love them. The Works has been replaced by a children's clothing store — a perfect fit for the Upper West Side. As clinically informative as the apps can be, I don't think there's a box to check that reads, "needs to relive childhood fantasy over, and over, *and over*."

What do I most regret *not* saying to Impossible? "What about me? What about what I want?" I didn't negotiate beforehand. If I had been smart, I should have said, "You know what? I'll trade you a Little Jimmy for a College Chris."

BISEXUAL STARTER PACK

by Kelli Trapnell

I am bisexual in a lot of ways. Like, yes, I like men, and I like women (and lots of people in between). But, I'm also full of other dualities. I am both a late bloomer and an early adopter. I lost my virginity early (15, to my best friend Melissa) and late (23, to my 8th serious boyfriend, Ryan). Growing up, I wasn't cool at all (at one point in time, I spoke pretty decent Elvish, having spent most of my time on JRR Tolkien webforums dedicated to parsing the language through close readings of *The Simarillion*), but I had some pretty badass moments. (I used to street race my mustang on Westheimer, Shepard and sometimes even I-10.) During freshman orientation at Texas Christian University, where I went for undergrad — a place both as rigidly conservative as you're imagining and also much more liberal than you'd think — everyone in my small group was asked to share our name, our hometown, and which song described us best. After thinking a moment, I answered with possibly the most bisexual song out there: "Bitch" by Meredith Brooks.

After a moment of stunned silence, my group leader asked me quietly if we could please avoid swearing from that point on. I had picked it because the song was about how the speaker — I guess Meredith Brooks? — was more than just one thing, more complicated than she appeared on the surface. And I picked it because Meredith Brooks sounded almost as confused as I felt going into undergrad as a closeted queer person with complicated feelings for my best friend and complicated feelings for my boyfriend.

Fast-forward four years to grad school in New York. Columbia University. It was a dream of mine, to move to the city and "make it as a writer," though I still wasn't sure what that meant. I had been at school for about half a year, and I'd made friends (something I'd struggled to do when I first came to New York with nothing but a bunch of just-ok stories and a shit ton of ambition). It was about as cliché as "Bitch," honestly, but we're all a little cliché when we're 18 and 21 and we haven't really lived at all yet. My friends at Columbia were so smart and worldly, brilliant writers who each had their own set of imagery the way that each of the X-Men had their own special power. Scott, my closest friend, was already out. He wrote high-society fiction, à la Edith Wharton, full of gowns and hors d'oeuvres on silver platters, laced with biting wit. Zalika wrote about growing up black in Toronto, her dialogue as sharp as a chef's knife every time two characters interacted. There was Rachel, who wrote stark, suburban teen dramas set against a perpetually burning California. Then there were Tim and Amber.

Tim loved Frank O'Hara poems, the idea that prose could be like jazz on the page, missing key elements on purpose, but not in an annoying way. (He was still working out that part of his style in the workshops we had together.) He was conventionally attractive — sandy brown hair, eyes the color of sunlight on hardwood floors and a wide, easy smile that broke into a laugh more often than not. He was kind and down to earth, despite his pretentious experimental prose ambitions — a rare find, to say the least, especially in art school. He often wrote about old TVs abandoned on the curb, friends who started out laughing at the same joke, then hardened against each other by the last page of the story. He was extremely anxious, which was why he smoked on the steps of Dodge Hall before every class. I instantly had a crush, and whenever I flirted with him, he flirted back.

Always smoking with him was one of my closer friends, Amber. Tim loved Amber. Amber was like me in that she wanted to write magical realism, slipstream, weird fiction — there was never a good name for it. The kind of prose where the usual bowl of clementines on the breakfast table might conduct electricity one morning, out of the blue. The kind of story that featured a girl who had implanted a whale's bone into her face, striving for some inane beauty standard, only to learn that the bone was blinding her, that the bone was vibrating to the plaintive call of its own kind whenever the girl walked along the shores of the fictional town where she lived. The kind of stories where magic was real and treacherous, or perhaps totally mundane compared to the stresses and the relationships of the human characters in the stories. In a word, both of us were writing stories which were confusing. Amber was from England, had gone to Cambridge where she spent her time flitting around — there is no other way to put it. Amber only ever flitted, in a pre-determined I-Will-Be-Your-Manic-Pixie-Dream-Girl-Dammit kind of concerted effort that looked stressful, at best. A mess, like me at that time. We were drawn to each other like magnets.

And, she had kissed girls before — something I had never done, despite the sex. Kissing had always been off the table. (But that's a story for another time.)

One night, I had the opportunity to read inside of a giant telescope on top of Pupin Hall, Columbia's astronomy hall. I read a piece about a woman obsessed with stars, who had allowed herself to become a mother and over the years had fallen out of love with everything but the stars in her backyard. Kind of a downer, honestly. But it went over well with the people in attendance, and when I stepped out onto the roof deck, Amber skipped over to me, tucked her hand behind my head and kissed me hard, on the mouth. My friend Scott's mouth dropped open, then widened into an excited smile. I was like him. I was 100% verified queer, even if I was more of a 60/40 when it came to liking girls vs. guys.

Suddenly I was navigating the coming out process, telling wider and wider groups of friends, losing some in the process. By the time spring break rolled around, when my whole friend group had decided to come to Texas with me, to see the rodeo and to run around on my family's farm together for inspiration, Tim and Amber and I found ourselves firmly planted in a serious love triangle. My bisexual starter pack, Scott liked to joke.

A few weeks before the trip, Zalika dropped out. Then Scott, and Rachel. I started to get nervous. What if it was just me and Tim and Amber out in the wilderness together? How would that work? (I was, and still am, thoroughly afraid of being in a thruple. For those of you who are ... bless you, you amazing, wonderful humans. I'm a Cancer, so I simply can't handle that many emotions and expectations at one time). Then Tim dropped out. I relaxed. So, everyone would drop out, and the trip would just be off. No problem. Probably better that way, honestly, now that everything had gotten so complicated.

But, no. Amber bought a plane ticket, full of excitement. At that point, we had been hooking up regularly after nights of too many drinks at Lionshead, the shitty dive bar where we all hung out three times a week, hoping to avoid working on our stories. "It'll be so fun!" she said, when I suggested maybe it wasn't such a good idea. I still wasn't out to my family at all — and she wasn't exactly the discreet type. "I want to go, please?"

At that point in my life, I was terrible at boundaries. So we went.

I'm sure you can imagine what happened, or some version of it, but you cannot possibly fathom how far underwater I felt when, as my religious sister drove me and Amber back to the farm from dinner through the pitch black night, Katy Perry's "I Kissed a Girl" came on the radio, and Amber said loudly, over the bubblegum song, "This is like Kelli's theme song right now!" Ice filled my chest as my sister asked, "What? Why?" and looked at me with uncertainty. I willed Amber to shut up, but she said, "Oh, because she just came out as bi."

We drove in silence the rest of the way home, and when we got to the farm, my sister and I hashed it out, her rather stunned, and me tearful and pleading. I wasn't ready, not by a long shot. Feelings of betrayal boiled inside of me, and Amber and I fought every day for the rest of the trip. When we got back to New York, I told her I needed some space and didn't talk to her for a month.

I should mention that during that time, Tim and I hooked up, and it was the most wonderfully satisfying casual sex of my life (the only casual sex of my life, to be honest — like I said, I'm a Cancer). We high-fived the next morning, then went to brunch and never needed to hook up again. Why spoil a golden thing?

We told Amber, out of courtesy, (again, no idea how to thruple) and she proceeded to put Tim in the dog house for another month. She already wasn't talking to me. Tim and I met once a week, for wings and beers at a neutral, non-MFA claimed sports bar in the area, so that he could talk through what Amber was fighting with him about that week. I was busy organizing the winter reading series — my friend Eddie and I were planning a Snow Ball-themed, truly extra night — where six current students would read. Tim warned me that Amber seemed pretty off the rails about us hooking up. "Still?" I asked. But he looked capital-C concerned.

Organizing the reading was part of my scholarship, so I couldn't get a replacement host. Plus, Eddie was counting on me. The night of the reading, I braced myself for whatever weird thing was about to go down and got dressed in my formal wear. Yes, formal wear.

By intermission, nothing strange had happened, and everyone was digging the vaguely Selena-esque ice queen fantasy we'd created (with Eddie, everything was vaguely Selena-esque, which I approved of). Amber was nowhere to be found, and neither was Tim.

Then, just as we were wrapping up intermission, I heard fighting in the stairwell. Tim, trying for a calming voice, Amber screaming back at him. Eddie tapped me. Time to get started.

I went up to the podium, even as the sounds of their fight traveled up into the hallway outside of the room where we were holding the reading, and as I was reading the bio for the first reader, Amber threw open the door and burst into the room, yanking her hand out of his wrist. It looked like she was holding something. She charged up to me where I was standing at the podium, and then the wind seemed to go out of her sails. "I was going to stab you," she said. "I thought about it."

Then she turned around and walked calmly out of the reading.

Obviously, we lost touch for a while. She and Tim got together and became a "thing," and I came out to my family. Over the next year, I started dating women for real, and I met Sarah, who had my heart after twenty minutes of talking and joking over fancy cocktails at a speakeasy in Astor Place. I knew I loved her more than anyone I'd ever met before the way that my heart hitched in my chest when I reached over to touch her hand. The way that I fell into her gray eyes and didn't want to swim out of them, ever. I handed my heart to her then and three and a half years later, I got down on one knee. We're getting married next fall, and I could not be happier.

A few months after the engagement, I got a message on Instagram from Amber. She's back in England now, and Scott, who's teaching in Spain, had the chance to see her. She's doing a lot better, he says. She's working on a book. Her message to me said, "I'm so proud of you, xx."

And you know what, at 30, I am, too.

FOR THE LOVE OF BENJI

by Jeffrey Marx

I'm showing my age here, but do you remember that cute dog Benji? He was a scrappy pup who had a bunch of movies in the '70s. He wandered in and out of people's lives, showing them that love was real and changing them for the better. Then, in the middle of the night, he would leave.

I love Benji, but Benji was a dick.

I met Joshua the second week I moved to LA at a mutual friend's birthday party. It was one of those parties with a swimming pool, a bunch of gay dudes, and really good molly. I had to lay down in a soft corner, and he glued himself to me. He was 12 years younger and not my usual type, but there was a deepness in his soul and magic in his eyes. Or maybe we were just on drugs. It was his first time and my 900th. We talked all night, and we made plans to hang that week.

"Is this a date date or just hanging out?" he asked after we ordered Thai food.

"It can be whatever you'd like!" I bounced it back to him, because I wanted to gauge his youthful intentions.

"I think I'd like it to be a date date!"

"Then me, too!"

"It's good to be clear," he said. "Too many times guys 'just hang out,' and then you never know who is thinking what. I hate trying to play mind-reader."

We went back to the studio apartment I had just moved into where he helped me paint an accent wall and put together IKEA furniture. We talked about music and movies, politics and religion. "I have a confession to make," he looked down on the ground and sighed a deep sigh that grew to be one of his signature mannerisms. "I come from a very devout Mormon family." We talked a little bit about what that was like.

"I have a confession to make myself," I said. "Does your family watch reality TV?"

"My mom and sister are obsessed with *Big Brother*."

"Well, they might actually know me from a similar show where I made a Mormon mom cry over gay marriage."

A few years previously, I had appeared on a reality TV show that no one watched except my mom and a bunch of Mormons. It was from that experience that I started working in casting, which led me to my new adventures in Los Angeles.

Mormons are a theme in my life. They always pop up in the strangest places ever since I went to Bible study with them my first year of college. The missionaries were hot, and I was thrilled that charming, all-American boys were inviting me somewhere. My mom thinks they keep getting brought into my life so I can learn how to be patient and kind, but I think I keep getting brought into theirs to wreck their world and trigger a crisis of faith, because they are drunk on stupidity.

Joshua and I fell in love fast. I had never dated someone with such an age gap, but it sort of made sense in the fiber of our relationship. He needed a gay mentor to make him watch *Showgirls* and explain the concept of camp; I needed a bright, hopeful heart while I started a new career in a new city. One night on my roof overlooking a homeless encampment in East Hollywood, he said "You know, introverts like me need extroverts like you because we have things to say, too! And you help me say things!" We got drunk at a gay bar for Valentine's Day where he said "I love you" first. He proudly insisted on holding my hand in public. We got annual passes to Disneyland because it was his favorite place. We called each other 'honey.' Eventually we brought our moms to meet at a Cheesecake Factory.

His mom definitely recognized me from the reality show. I could tell by the way we never talked about the reality show. She was a controlling nightmare and never expected her gay son's gay boyfriend to be an older, fatter, smarter man. Can you imagine explaining what a chubby chaser is to a Mormon lady? Needless to say, we didn't get along, and Joshua sort of loved it. He had been staying at her place while he looked for work, and she flat out bullied him about dating me. He got really stressed out, and, after only six months of dating, he moved into my studio apartment. Talking about our hopes and dreams while cuddling in our tiny Harry Potter closet made being poor and constantly between gigs seem not as terrible. The next six months were the most sweet and adorable I've ever spent with anyone.

Then one of his friends invited us to an orgy for New Year's Eve. Although Joshua offered to be monogamous when we had our first relationship talk, we decided to have an open relationship. I knew that being 25 years old and having his recovering, religiously-oppressed sexuality blasting everywhere, it would be impractical. We had one rule: if the guy was rude to me, I would use my power of veto. Shady assholes don't get to sleep with boyfriends. Joshua agreed. We got invited upstairs to one of the play rooms. "I brought my gear! You guys should check it out!"

Gear?

They reached into their duffle bags and revealed several custom-made leather puppy masks. They put them on over their heads, reached back into the bags and pulled out a long, black object. One end was a dildo that would go in your butthole, and the other end looked like a puppy tail. They attached a leather harness across their chests and inserted the tails. They got on all fours and started sniffing each other and howling. Joshua tried on a hood and dove right in. As the only human in the room, the pups kept bouncing over to me to get scratches behind the ears. They frolicked with each other until one of them motioned for me to whip out my dick. I did, and they all started sucking it. Later they would say, "doggies like bones."

It turned into a very long night, and Joshua was electrified. I could tell that the effects of the Mormon cult were being lifted. We had sex twice when we got home. As humans. In deep, human love.

He started searching out the leather puppy scene online. Over the course of the next year, I let him explore with very little boundaries. A close eye and a long leash. A guy here or there got vetoed, but, overall, it was a good arrangement. Sometimes he would go into what was called "headspace" around the house, and I would act as his "handler," throwing squeaky dog toys and giving him pets and calling him a "good boy." Then he told me he found someone who did hypnotherapy over Skype who was also a handler. That was weird, but, OK. I'm a cool boyfriend!

I didn't know how to navigate the world we were getting pulled into. It was a lot of young men who had been broken in some way, reclaiming their power through this interesting therapy tool. Lots of stories of religious families, addiction, and body issues. Power and control dynamics were inherently woven into the system, so it was the kind of culture where it was easy for predators to hide in the open. There were a fair amount of older, lecherous opportunists who wanted to be pup masters. See, there was a hierarchy in that world. A pup could have pup brothers, alphas, and betas. A pup also could have a handler or a master or an owner. Sometimes they got collared, which was the act of taking an actual dog collar from, like, PetSmart, and locking it so that they couldn't get it from around their necks. I played along and bought a dog tag with his pup name and my phone number. You know, in case he got lost, people could call me? He named himself Pup Sassy. He had a sharp wit for being kept in the Mormon closet for so long. He cried when I gave him the tag. My heart melted.

One night he brought me to a puppy seminar. It was taught by a man in his 40s. "The first time I was introduced to puppy play, I was 14 years old and my 23 year old boyfriend stripped me down naked, put a leash on me, and marched me outside. I knew then I was a pup." I couldn't quite pay attention the rest of the night after that tale of sexual abuse, which no one else seemed to register as such.

We did a trip to Palm Springs with a mixed group of friends. The handler of one of Joshua's puppy friends whipped out his cock at a gay bar that wasn't really that kind of gay bar and put his hand on the back of my boyfriend's head to get him to suck it. I flipped out. They all ditched me to go back to the hotel. I flipped out again. Every time those puppy people were around, something would go wrong.

We were still in love. We hated when we would fight, and we'd want to make up as soon as possible. It never felt good going to bed mad at each other, so we always talked it out. "What can I do to be a better honey?" His response: "Fill the ice trays." He asked if I could see us getting married someday, if I wanted kids. (I could. And not necessarily.)

Over Christmas break we went to New York City. I planned to propose to him under the Rockefeller tree because he has a certain fascination with things that light up. I was gonna say "Well, you love things that light up — and you light me up! Wanna get married?" But, when we went to the tree after the Rockettes show, it was turned off for some reason. A big, dark, empty Christmas tree. I took that as a sign and got cold feet. I still have the engraved dog tag I was gonna propose with instead of a ring.

I was working long hours, and he was spending more and more time with his pack. They had jacuzzis and home-made sex dungeons in the garage. How could I compete? Especially when his circle of lost boys would say things like "You're not getting the full experience unless your boyfriend is into this, too" or "You're not a real pup unless you have a handler."

I took him to see one of my favorite singers, Jenny Lewis and The Watson Twins. They were performing the entire *Rabbit Fur Coat* album in a cute church. He had never heard of them and was enthralled. It was a good date night. He asked about us looking for a bigger apartment soon. I said yes, let's make that work. It was a very romantic evening, and we cuddled ourselves to sleep. Often his last words before he'd fall asleep were "You make me feel safe. I love you."

He had nightmares a lot. I would just touch his arm so our bodies would remember the electricity of love and hopefully change his bad dreams into good.

The next day, he picked a fight with me about a shady gay I had vetoed (the handler from Palm Springs who forced a public blow job and would only talk about how he used to be in porn and whatever he heard on Rachel Maddow the night before). When Joshua came home later that afternoon, something wasn't right. Through genuine tears, he told me that he wanted to explore a new kind of relationship and find a real handler. He said he didn't have anyone in mind. He wanted to be free to find someone. I asked why one day he would talk about moving into a bigger place together and the next break up with me. I hate trying to play mind-reader. "Honestly, I don't know what I want, and maybe I'm making a huge mistake, but this is what I have to do right now."

Joshua started doing laundry with the laundry quarters that I always made sure were available. I'd make special trips to the bank for rolls of quarters. I wondered if he ever noticed the automatically refilling mug of coins? I never asked him for money because I know how hard it is to be young and barely make anything. I kept thinking: YOUR LAUNDRY IS FREE! I AM YOUR HANDLER! He moved all his things out of the apartment that night. It took me two months to stop crying. He chased me down, and he let me go. I didn't argue, because when you love someone you're supposed to set them free or whatever, right? You want them to be happy, even if not being with you anymore is what makes them happy.

In my eyes, he traded the oppressive Mormon church for a different kind of cult. At least in this one you get to do drugs and suck dick! But if you're not part of their sex-focused club, they push you out for the crime of being independent and secure in your own skin. I never clicked with the toxic masculinity clique, and if I heard one more leather bro in a biker costume complain about drag queens being too effeminate, I was gonna choke on the hypocrisy. It's just a different kind of drag, baby. So through ugly tears, I wished Joshua the best and told him if he ever felt alone he could call me. Off he scampered to live with the shady gay handler and his collection of pups who undoubtedly helped him form his escape plan from our relationship.

About four months later, I got a call out of the blue on a Sunday morning. One of his pup friends left him alone at a rave where he was doing acid for the first time. When the sun came up and the party had ended, Benji sat in his car and wondered what to do. So he called me. We had a funny chat for about an hour, and I lifted his spirits out of the dark acid hole until he was able to drive home safely.

Another whole year went by, and we barely wished each other Happy Birthday on social media. It was very difficult for me to have loved so deeply just to have it gutted in a flash by a pack of literal hyenas. When you have the love of Benji and he leaves in the middle of the night, there's a moment where you are forced to ask yourself if the love was ever real? It was real. It was just also temporary. Soak in the good moments because you never know what's around the corner.

I ran into Benji and his new boyfriend at a bar. Turns out he didn't live with the creepo handler anymore, and all his pups left him for being overbearing. (Justice!) The new boyfriend had amazing energy and instantly seemed like a good human being. My heart was happy to know they were doing well and not part of that poisonous circle that strangled our love. I was astounded to learn that even after all the heartbreak, I was very happy and forgiving. I wasn't jealous or sad or wistful. Once you've truly loved someone, they become part of your emotional DNA, and it finally felt good to reconnect and officially move forward. After a few drinks, I called myself a Lyft and hugged them goodbye. I couldn't help but notice Joshua took a deep sniff of my neck and hugged me a little tighter than I hugged him.

Good boy.

THE ROYAL WEDDING

by Veronica Garza

It was the morning of May 28, 2018, and an international news article just outed my girlfriend. I was waking up in London with dozens of text messages from friends saying: "Look at you!" "You and Leslie look great!" "Oh shit, you've gone international!"

An MSNBC article had just called my girlfriend and I "Royal Superfans." That felt great for about a minute until I scrolled to the end of the article spilling the beans on my not-yet-out-of-the-closet partner.

What did I just do?

Back in the winter of 2017, I felt like a champion. My girlfriend of one year, Leslie, and I were planning our second trip together. At 34 years of age, it was the first healthy relationship I'd ever been in. It was crazy. I'd say something, and she'd listen. When she's say something, I'd listened. And then we got to have sex. This shit was great.

Before Leslie, I used to think there was no one out there for me. There was the girl that said I wasn't a real lesbian because I had too many emotions (I mean, isn't a lesbian relationship ALL EMOTIONS?); there was that one time I dated a 24-year-old, and if I didn't talk about Harry Potter, I lost her attention; and let's not forget the woman who, after her second failed marriage and now on her third to a woman, mentioned *I* didn't seem like a long-term partner. After all that disappointment, of course, I was dejected. And, believe me, I know dejection. I'm a Cowboys fan.

It's not that I don't have my own flaws. I love sports. I know, as a lesbian, that's not a very controversial opinion. But, growing up an athlete, I struggled to learn how to share failures and losses as a team. I was always silently keeping score, making sure I knew somehow I was still winning. I kept tallying the points in the never-ending game of Veronica vs. Life.

And I didn't like to lose. That competitive spirit probably at least partially fueled my interest in stand-up. The other contributing factor was having an excuse never to stop joking around, something Leslie learned to tolerate, if not be completely charmed by. So, when I presented the idea of going to London during Royal Wedding weekend, I assumed she would realize I was 100 percent fucking with her. Even I wasn't expecting what would happen next.

The entire room fell silent — the type of silence that overtakes an audience at a tennis match as they wait for a player to serve. She didn't say anything for about 15 seconds, and then she responded, "That sounds fun."

I spat out a tiny bit of my wine.

"You serious?"

"Yes, and maybe we can go get fish & chips?" Leslie added.

OK, I gotta admit, that was one point for Leslie.

We had a great rest of the dinner, but I was too scared to bring it up again. The following February, I was at work and in the middle of telling my boss the plot to the third *50 Shades* movie, when I got a text that read, "Tickets are booked! Royal Wedding get ready! Leslie and Veronica are coming!"

I had three ginger teas that morning, so I was already extremely hyped. Fueled by love, and adrenaline, I wanted, no, needed to take it to social media.

"Attention: @houseofwindsor … get ready, Royal Wedding 2019 ... Brooklyn's coming!"

"Attention @meghanmarkle" (Is this really her Twitter handle? I still don't know.)

"@suits @USA get ready ... Brooklyn's coming!"

"Attention @rowanatkinson @mrbean @bbc1 @bbc2 @bbc3 @skinsUK @devpatel ... get ready, Brooklyn's coming!"

"Attention @davidbeckham @victoriabeckham … get ready, Brooklyn's coming, and I'm not talking about your son @BrooklynBeckham!"

I don't usually pride myself on my tweets, but that series was an opus in 144-character movements.

Leslie and I planned the trip and were both super excited. I researched all that I could about British culture. I studied tea etiquette (you aren't supposed to put your pinky up when you drink it, you fool); I watched a documentary about the Royal Family (did you know they are not allowed to play Monopoly?); I watched *The IT Crowd* (which has nothing to do with the royal family, but Richard Ayoade is a treasure).

In early May I received a tweet from a reporter at MSNBC. It read:

"@veros_broke I saw you plan to attend the royal wedding in May. We are writing an article about Royal Superfans and I would love to chat with you about your plans to visit during that weekend."

ARE YOU SERIOUS? Of course! I messaged her back with my contact information, and I let her know it didn't matter when she called me, I'd make myself available. We had the call, and I confirmed that we were indeed going to London during that time. I was certain to mention that I am Texan, Mexican-American and gay, to assure that I would get a mention in the article. We had a long conversation about my mom's adoration for Princess Diana; how unbelievable the whole moment was; how a non-royal and person of color will finally be a part of this family. The conversation was quick, but I talk fast, so I got everything out that I needed.

All I could think was how I couldn't wait to see Leslie's face when I was mentioned in this article. She might have gotten us to London, but I had arrived — in print!

One point for Veronica.

Almost 48 hours passed before the reporter reached back out and asked if I was available to meet up with a couple of other Royal Superfans (which I shall now only refer to as *RSFs,* even in everyday conversation) prior to the wedding. I asked if I could bring my girlfriend. Everything was set for Wednesday when we all met in front of Buckingham Palace.

Up until that point, I had never been to Europe, so I was having a rough time containing my excitement. Every now and then I would yell, "London, baby!" like that two-part season finale of *Friends* where Ross marries Emily despite saying the wrong name at the altar. (Side note: What the fuck, Ross?)

We headed towards Buckingham Palace, and I managed to find the reporter among the sea of tourists. We started the group introduction: there was a mom and daughter from Texas, a fellow Brooklynite named Christina, and one woman who didn't want us to forget she lived in Manhattan. I will call her "pageantry" because she did not stop telling us how she used to compete in beauty pageants. I have relatively little experience and knowledge of that world, but I do know that there are two types of people who participate in beauty pageants — those who won and those who tell people they competed. She was the latter. Did I mention she told me her TV credits?

We took photos in front of Buckingham Palace and got interviewed. The reporter asked me about my enthusiasm for the Royal Family and how the trip transpired. Leslie shared the backstory, and the reporter laughed hard at Leslie's enthusiasm.

Another point for Leslie. You always get points when you make a woman laugh.

The Saturday morning of the Royal Wedding, I woke up and checked my phone. Five different friends had sent me a link to an MSNBC article titled "Royal Super Fans Flock To London For Royal Wedding." (Look it up, it's hilarious.) I scrolled down, and there was a lovely pic of me and Leslie taking a selfie. I scrolled down further and see myself credited as a "Brooklyn-based Mexican-American stand-up comedian." (Hello, that's a credit.) I had a few quotes in there.

Then I realized, Leslie's name is in the article ... as my partner.

Push pause on Tegan & Sara's "Closer" for a quick moment: Leslie wasn't out to her parents yet. She wasn't out to all her family, except for a select few.

I handed the phone to Leslie. She didn't say a thing. She was making that cute frown she makes when she does math, or when she's into the song that's playing at the grocery store, that coincidentally is the same frown she makes when she's upset with me. I began to wonder if I should look for an AirBnB in the area just for myself.

What if the same day Harry and Meghan marry is the same day I get dumped?

I hadn't said a word, and neither had she. After what I assumed had been a full day, I asked if she was going to be okay.

She responded, "Well, if they didn't know, now they know."

The girl lived in Brooklyn for one year, and suddenly she was quoting Biggie lyrics.

Leslie tells me how we are a couple and that my win is her win; her win is my win; together we win. She just came out on the international stage to her family, and she's still able to just shrug it off. Is this what an emotionally healthy adult looks like?

Ten points for Leslie.

I know, I know, the moral of the story is that it's not about winning, but even I have to concede this one. There's no way, after seeing how she handled that, that I could ever doubt she was the G.O.A.T. So, while millions watched a non-royal break tradition and marry a prince, in another part of London, I had my own break in protocol. Celebrating this win, OUR win, together with Leslie, I've never felt more like royalty.

SPIRIT

Do you have one of those places where you walk in and instantly feel like you belong? Maybe it's a favorite café or Disney World or a comic book convention. (For me, it's the LUSH Cosmetics in Union Square.) It's a place where you feel you can relax into your truest self among people who understand you. In a way, it feels like home.

Our queer ancestors huddled together in speakeasies and created complex codes to find one another and share that experience. Today, we have the ability to conjure that sense of home across physical distance. Maybe you felt it reading one of these essays. It's that sudden shock of familiarity, like running into your exact doppelgänger at the LUSH Cosmetics in Union Square — a total stranger who somehow feels like family.

It's like tapping into a collective queer consciousness, and, when it happens, it's exhilarating. These final two essays celebrate those otherworldly, magical threads that bind us over space and time, the shared spirit that defines us as a community.

THE AGE OF INNOCENCE

by David Odyssey

What you have to understand about the time is this: Bush was president. If the Twin Towers went down when I was in sixth grade, that means that Bush was *still* president through high school, the fall of Weezer, and the first four seasons of *One Tree Hill*. He was president when I heard Estelle's "American Boy" for the first time in the summer of 2008, on the drive to Jewish summer camp, where I'd lose my virginity in the Arts and Crafts room.

George Bush was president for a very long time. And he shattered me, shattered all gay boys. The end of my first decade on this earth — the '90s — was the final feast for queer children. It was a surge of sugar and sex and lurid satire, a neon Jenga tower of self-aware culture, built on *Scream* and Gracie Lou Freebush and *MADTV* and *Spice World*. And it made sense to me, for a while. Daddy Clinton wasn't being entirely forthcoming with us, but neither were my parents when I asked them anything about their divorce, about why we left Israel when I was born, about why my brother went to prison when I was eight. But it didn't matter, because I had delicious distractions: sleepovers, pool parties, *Sailor Moon*, and Holly Marie Combs.

And then there was 2000, and 2001, and the straight people won. Everything turned gray and starchy, like gulag gruel in movies about men. We couldn't make fun of our new daddy, the president, George Bush. We had to do what he said. We had to believe in America, not as the consumerist terror-Tokyo of *Josie and the Pussycats*, but as an idea, or something. And then time started spilling over. My stepdad died, my mom started passing out drunk during our *Buffy* nights, my dad grew a beard, there was a war, or two wars (?), Destiny's Child split up, and all the boys I'd forced to watch *Supergirl* with Faye Dunaway at my eighth birthday party were now wearing baggy pants and listening to Eminem. I gained weight and wore oversized *Dragon Ball Z* t-shirts. Left-Eye died in Honduras, my summer camp counselors made fun of Britney Spears' Vegas wedding, and I hated them for it. Harry Potter had mood swings. I thought I would die, or be kicked out of the house, or kill myself. My parents were vacant, my brothers idiots, and I was willing myself not to hit puberty, lest I turn into a dick-grabbing, racist swine like every other boy in my class. I would cleave to my *Buffy* reruns on FX and my *Teen Titans* comic books.

I endured, and adapted, as we went through Bush's second term. I survived MySpace, two rounds of Accutane, a protracted Hot Topic phase, Nickelback, Nelly Furtado, and my dad buying me a Ford F150, to come out new and clean and positive. It was the summer of 2008 when I graduated high school. Obama's star was rising. There was a new bad girl anthem called "I Kissed A Girl" that didn't sound like those Pussycat Dolls. I was no longer a child, but certainly not a man. I was a twink.

I was off to Israel for my gap year before college — I'd be with my camp friends, in my birthplace, where I could go out legally, and I could reconnect with my family. It was a time of unsteady rebirth, the first harvest after seven years of fallow ground. There were no divas, no pop icons, no discourse on anything beyond *The Dark Knight* and Sarah Palin. No swiping, no stories, no think pieces. I really liked *Battlestar Galactica* and short bathing suits and hanging out with my mom. The rest was wide open. I didn't know how much of myself had been shut away, kept entombed, untouched. I wasn't fully there.

And so, after a decade of stunted, suburban dissociation that would require a *later* decade of therapy, self-help, and Al-anon meetings to break down, I was surprised to find myself … *living* in Tel Aviv. Call it a motherland bond, an ancestral reckoning, or simply a cosmopolitan reawakening after 18 years in Texas, but the air I breathed there was different. And I knew it was special to me. Unlike the other 18 year olds on my trip, I wasn't content to sit around with other Americans. I wanted to be in the city. I was bone-thin, dead sober, and terrified of sustained sexual contact, but lacked any vocabulary to process it. That would come later. At that time, all I could do, all I wanted to do, was dance.

And so it was with the touch of destiny that I found a flyer for Glam-ou-Rama. It was some sort of party, designed with the taste level of Barbie's Dream House. "POP/KITSCH!" it read, along with this quote:

"The good end happily and the bad unhappily; that is what fiction means." —Oscar Wilde.

Who knows what I wore that first night. But I grabbed some straight girls and went to the spot: Culture Club. Could it be anywhere else? We met the gate-keeper, a beautiful sphinx called Asaf, whom we called the Silver Fairy. And, immediately, Glam-ou-Rama became my bliss, my rebirth, my Jerusalem away from the real one.

Upon entering, I looked through the crowd and saw, projected on the wall, the bobbing blonde head of Paris Hilton. It was her sex tape, *1 Night in Paris*. And the soundtrack? Geri Halliwell's cover of "It's Raining Men." I got it: if you threw it all together, the past was a laughable travesty, a mess that had to be laughed off, a camp masterpiece. Yes, the trauma was real, but what power did it have when set to the *Bridget Jones' Diary* soundtrack?

Glam-ou-Rama was, indeed, a kitsch party: when the A*Teens' cover of "Gimme! Gimme! Gimme! (A Man After Midnight)" came on, it was met with hosiahs. It was not a space for irony, or drag, or post-modern recollection. We came to dance with love for Jennifer Lopez, Britney Spears, Republica, Ciara, for the ones who had helped us survive to that point.

In a militant state with an island mentality, that is how the gays processed. Gaza, the Holocaust, the rocket fires, the corrupt prime ministers … of course, the response had to be as subtle as a Katy Perry video. What they knew, in the insanity of their circumstances, was this: there is no innocence — not for gay boys who unknowingly enter a merciless sexual economy the moment their skin clears up; not for queer girls who want to dye their hair and protest their apartheid state; not for me, whose body and mind had been taken away from him at too young an age. So we'd reclaim it, manufacture it, double-down on it in its purest form. And we'd be in on the joke, smiling at each other like Rachel Griffiths and Toni Collette in *Muriel's Wedding*.

I danced so hard at Glam-ou-Rama that my glasses would slide off my nose. I'd scream Sporty's closing lyrics to "Who Do You Think You Are?" until I was hoarse. I kissed a lot of boys, but wouldn't do much else, and that was OK. We wore costumes for every themed edition of the party — Fairy Tale Masquerade, the Spice party, Paris Hilton's Bitch Ball — but it was for our enjoyment; the technology of stories didn't exist yet.

How good it felt to be silly, to do things because they felt and sounded good, to not see some artificial elegance in being jaded. 2009 was approaching. Beyoncé resurged and "Single Ladies" was everywhere. But there was no discourse, no tiresome *Jezebel* pieces about it written by white women, no performative affirmations of her work. We just liked doing the dance moves from the music video.

I was a skinny, silly, styleless faggot. Nobody was watching. Nobody cared. No pithy captions were needed. No grand stage. No follower base. I didn't have a history, or a future. Just late nights dancing to S Club 7 and walking back to my grandmother's apartment, praying I could sneak in before she'd wake up at 6 a.m. Of course, I'd never win: one of her neighbors would call her later and tell her that they'd seen lights on in the apartment late at night — had there been a burglar? She'd smell my clothes, which were hexed with the deep stench of (other men's) cigarettes and (other men's) cologne. And when I'd stumble out of bed at 10 a.m., she'd be on the phone with her friend Genya, talking shit about me in Hebrew, then, when I'd pick up on it, Yiddish, and, when I'd pick up on that, Polish.

She taught me conversational Hebrew, or at least the warped conversational Hebrew of a Polish Holocaust survivor who only kept to her own. We formed a relationship that was ours, liminal, delicate, caught between languages. It was a bond that could only gather in an unplanned, unobserved, innocent way. There wasn't much to show for it, which made it even sweeter to enjoy.

I'd sit on her couch for hours, begging her not to cook, watching music videos on MTV Europe. Katy Perry, "Hot & Cold;" Ciara, "Love Sex Magic;" Britney Spears, "Womanizer;" Kelly Rowland, "Work."

As spring came, it was clear that a new era was forming, that the blissful ambiguity must give way to something new. The first moments of morning were over, it was time for a new day and all the work that entailed. And so the age must have a herald, a diva. She came in the form of an Italian girl from New York with a protruding schnoz and glaring blonde bangs. She was Lady Gaga, and we, the self-proclaimed Pop Sluts of Glam-ou-Rama, elected her as godhead.

I listened to "Love Game" every day, and replayed "I Like It Rough" while unboxing rainbow pride flags at my internship at the Tel Aviv Gay and Lesbian Center. Life was starting to have a new texture, music was coming into a new milieu, and the current incarnation of myself was taking shape. I was speaking Hebrew fluently. The Silver Fairy considered me a friend. Safta and I were thick as thieves. Obama was charging ahead. I wanted to make sure my lightning bolt makeup was just perfect for the Night of a Thousand Gagas party.

By summer, after Pride, I would head back to the States, where I'd long for Tel Aviv from my dreary, provincial dorm room. We'd continue in the direction we'd agreed on, bigger and better. *The Fame* would become *The Fame Monster*. Beyoncé's every move would become a polemic. Robyn would reinvent the genre. We'd regroup, regrow, and become a fully operational queer culture system again, with the growing pains of *Glee* and Dan Savage.

And we'd become bitter again, jaded, resentful of Obama and Lena Dunham and *ARTPOP*. I'd hitch myself to identities, to careers, to dreams, to little avail. I'd go back to Tel Aviv every summer, to jumbo-sized Glam-ou-Ramas, souped up at mega-clubs in celebration of Gaga's latest releases. I'd hear IconaPop for the first time and levitate to Kylie Minogue's "Timebomb." Safta would start to lose her memory, and we'd be joined by loving caregivers for endless, repetitive conversations. Netanyahu would become a long-term dictator. My friends would get married and stay in Texas.

By 2014, the Peter Pan years had come to an end, or at least I wanted them to. I moved to New York City. I wanted to prove to myself that I existed, that I was defined by something. I could no longer abide by the blissful ambiguity of the beginning.

Soon, there'd be another fall. Trump, Harvey Weinstein, Kavanaugh. My repressed memories of my brother, of his violence, his misogyny. The light of an iPhone camera illuminated everything — our identities, our potential, but also our violations, our denial. It's a new age, one we don't understand. So we do what we always have done: we cling to Kim Petras, and Carly Rae Jepsen, and paint the sky in glitter.

It is a decade since the first Glam-ou-Rama parties, and I think I understand. For the delicate ones, the angels, the little boys who make collages and watch music videos all day, there is no childhood but the one we make for ourselves. We let the president and our mothers and fathers and brothers believe differently, because they'll never know how pure it is, and how precious. And so we affirm eternal youth, like Willy Wonka, and the gaudier the better. Some of us do it with bodies, and beauty, and the blur of sex and stories. And some of us do it with bright colors and happy songs, the

Pointer Sisters, and kissing boys on the dancefloor. And it is there, in that most sacred of space, that once-an-eclipse dance party, that we reveal it, that treasure thought lost for centuries, occluded to the unworthy, that thing they thought they scrubbed away but they never even touched, that pink lightning that surges through us, in abundance, that which belongs to us by birthright. We were innocent, and so can be again, whenever we choose, forever and ever.

DRAG REVEALS

by Zach Zimmerman

1.

In a Wal-mart dressing room in 2007, a shy freshman tried on a black bra, a black dress, and a red wig. The attendant looked on in dismay. A few hours later, he entered a college drag competition with too little clothing on his body and too much Everclear in his body. He was never fully dressed without a shot. Over-inebriated and uninhibited, he took to the runway. He danced. He danced and danced. He danced in the sacred way only a 19-year-old Southern Baptist whose body knows he's queer before his mind does can. A nipple reveal in the final round clinched the title: I won.

Two years later, two weeks before Valentine's Day 2009, RuPaul debuted her drag competition, which means *RuPaul's Drag Race* came out before I did. My only out gay friend, an Adonis who manicured his eyebrows the same way God must've manicured his genes, invited me to watch the premiere. I said no. I didn't know why. Not interested? Still a foot in the closet? How many choices do we make consciously, and how many are hazy, dressed up in logic after the fact? Or maybe I was just lazy.

2.

I watched my first episode of *Drag Race* for the same reason anyone does anything they don't want to do: a very cute boy. I had dodged the show for a decade. A chance choice gave way to inertia, and unchecked inertia became identity. Eventually, I was so far behind, the only way for this queen to win Hearts was to shoot the moon. So I hadn't watched the race at all.

The Very Cute Boy asked me where I'd be watching the Season 10 premiere. I had just moved to New York, where drag — and my dodging of it — seemed to matter more. I named the only gay bar I could think of.

Therapy is a Hell's Kitchen gay bar where the bars are hidden like Easter eggs on the day Jesus rose from the dead. I'd been there once before, when I went home with a man who controlled his apartment lighting with his watch, a fact I learned when he woke me up to kick me out at 3 a.m. So on a cold Thursday right before Easter 2018, I arrived at Therapy to watch my first episode of *Drag Race*.

I quickly learned there'd be no flirting during the show. Chit-chat was self-policed by 100 gay men trying to see and hear the show projected onto a screen. During commercial breaks, the TV audio feed was cut much to the dismay of advertisers across America and replaced with a local drag queen's commentary. I couldn't keep up with the references.

On my first date with The Very Cute Boy the following week, we saw the gay high school rom-com *Love, Simon.* I over-sympathized with the villain who was a high school mascot. The Very Cute Boy did not. When conversation turned to *Drag Race*, I was proud that I'd seen an episode.

"You've seen one episode?"

Turns out only brushing your teeth the night before a dentist visit is not an effective oral hygiene regimen. Once is not enough.

There was not a second date.

3.

Alyssa Edwards was a contestant on the fifth season of *RuPaul's Drag Race* and quickly became a fan favorite. The smooth Southern talker and trained dancer with a penchant for non-sequiturs and a signature "tongue pop," didn't win the competition, but she won the war: a return to an *All-Stars* season and a spin-off Netflix series about her dance studio in Texas.

I learned all this in the 24 hours between being asked to open for Alyssa Edwards at Caroline's on Broadway and opening for Alyssa Edwards at Caroline's on Broadway. In a Google haze, I mined my material for broad appeal gay jokes, penned new drag jokes, and furiously texted my *Drag Race* fan friends for a download on who she was and what she was about. My not watching *Drag Race* was biting me in the ass in a bad way.

I arrived at the venue a half hour before the first show. I was terrified Alyssa would make a reference I wouldn't get, and I'd be immediately fired. I was also convinced we'd become best friends. In reality, I spent more time with the bouncer outside her dressing room. As the venue started to fill up with gay men, female fans, and their very supportive straight husbands, I got nervous. Would I be outed as a *Drag Race* denier? A blasphemer? A guest pastor introducing a god I didn't worship?

I did my 10 minutes, said Alyssa's name a lot (the trick to opening for anyone), and introduced her video. Stars play videos before they go on stage. Her pre-recorded voice gave way to a microphone off-stage.

"Hello, Caroline's!"

The audience sprang to their feet like a reverse death drop. They clapped and hollered and clapped and hollered, and I sat in the back in awe of it all. She made a joke, the audience died; she made a reference, they died again. I didn't get the inside jokes, but I knew she was killing, and my cheeks hurt from smiling along. I was in the room, but apart; in the community, but a witness to the spectacle.

Alyssa (and I) did five shows that weekend. I watched religious rapture each time.

Before the final show, her assistant came over to me.

"Alyssa wants you to wear this." He handed me an 8-foot blue boa. I'd been told I was hired since I was "gay, but not too fabulous" but now the queen herself was asking me to wear something a bit more queer. I took the stage, the blue queer snake exposing me to the knowledge of good and evil, a first-hand witness of the cult of celebrity of *Drag Race* fandom, as my body remembered the black bra from Wal-Mart.

4.

The mainstream popularity of *RuPaul's Drag Race* gave rise to DragCon events, multi-day conventions with panels and paid meet and greets, since 2015. But since 2012 though, there's been an alternative drag festival in Brooklyn called Bushwig. At DragCon, you can get a T-shirt with a famous drag queen's catchphrase; at Bushwig, you can watch a duo lip sync "Am I A Man or Am I a Muppet?" set to a fisting sequence.

A queer friend had hyped the fest to me as an accepting, queer utopia all year, so I bought my ticket and saved the date. I wanted to be a part of the Brooklyn queer community, and I was willing to show up for the festival. Unsure what to wear, I donned some haphazard collection of a black mesh tank and random ropes ("Random rope play is not safe," a festival goer reprimanded me) and put some of my friend's makeup on ("You look like that meme of the young girl with bad eye shadow and bad lipstick," a friend pointed out).

After a few shows and enough vodka-Red Bulls to feel fully dressed like college, another performer took the stage and the audience erupted in a rapture I'd seen before. Nina West had just been baptized into RuPaul's TV empire, and while the crowd certainly supported their edgy, local queens, no one is immune to celebrity.

When her number began, nostalgia tore through the crowd. A Disney medley. Song clips from *The Lion King*, *The Little Mermaid*, *Beauty and the Beast*, and double *Mulan* were paired with quick-change outfits from each iconic princess. Recognizable chords and color patterns awoke a secular chorus of queers in the Bushwick warehouse. Everyone sang along, having rehearsed the songs in the carpeted living rooms of the '90s when Love, Simon, Drag and Race were just words. Old was made new through a lip sync, the recitation of our secular Bible verses, fringe gospels that have helped forge a new queer canon and community.

I didn't plan to cry during a Disney medley at a drag festival, but I did. I cried at the community that stood around me, reclaiming the musical telegrams we memorized as kids, not knowing we'd one day recite them to each other as someone lip synced them back to us. I cried at the coming together of people who were left out, the queens and high school mascots and drag divas.

I cried for the nostalgia I missed because of the culture I'd banished: what my Adonis friend and The Very Cute Boy must feel when they watch *Drag Race*, what the five crowds felt for Alyssa, what the room felt for Nina. Drag divas and pop princesses serving gender-bends and death drops, constructions and destructions and presentations and provocations, tucks and twists and boobs and butt pads, wrinkled dollar bills and smokey eyes, audio juxtapositions and compositions, camp and cartoons.

I cried because I realized culture is work. It's easier not to watch 12 seasons of a TV show. It's easier to opt out than keep up. It's easier to be lazy. And when you grew up feeling on the fringe, it's easier to reject the invitation to come inside … to watch that new show, to brave the crowded bar, to keep up.

I cried as nostalgia washed over me and washed over me, like applause, like community, like sweat at a freshman year drag ball when things were ever clear.

About the Editor

Bobby Hankinson (he/him) is a Brooklyn-based writer, performer, creative, and full-time homosexual. He founded Kweendom in 2015 as a live LGBTQ comedy and storytelling show, which TimeOut NY described as "consistently dope." In addition to performing across the country, Bobby is pop-culture columnist for leading LGBTQ website Towleroad.com. His work has appeared in the Boston Globe, Houston Chronicle, VICE, Gothamist, and more. He shares his humble party palace with his partner/best friend, Nathan, and a 6lb rescue dog named Carly Rae Jepsen.

About the Authors

Kevin Allison (he/him) has created all kinds of stories, with his writing and acting work on the legendary sketch comedy series *The State* on MTV, as well as *Reno 911!, Flight of the Conchords, High Maintenance,* Blue Man Group, and much more. In 2009, Kevin created RISK!, the live show and audio podcast where people tell true stories they never thought they'd dare to share. The podcast is now downloaded over 1 million times per month. Kevin is also the author of the hit book, *RISK! True Stories People Never Thought They'd Dare To Share,* which was published by Hachette Books in 2018. As the founder of The Story Studio in New York, Kevin has coached bestselling authors, well-known comedians, and brilliant teachers and executives from a wide spectrum of fields.

Danny Artese (he/him) is a New York City storyteller who grew up in the conservative southern California suburb of Orange County, not far from Sweet Valley High, as he likes to believe. He is a Moth GrandSLAM winner who has also appeared on RISK!, The Story Collider, and The Moth Radio Hour. He has written and performed the solo show *Mama Said I'd Be Gay Like This* and hosts/produces the storytelling series The Day I Should Have. He has the unique distinction of having shared stages with both Tim Gunn and the band Vomit Fist. Danny encourages you to tell your story because sharing our stories reminds us that we're not as alone as we might think.

Jeena Bloom (she/her) is a transgender female standup comedian and writer. She divides her time between Los Angeles and New York City, while also performing stand-up comedy all over the world. Her past appearances include Comedy Central, New York Magazine, and Vice. She has had five different hair colors over the past two years.

Jamie Brickhouse (he/him) is the author of the critically acclaimed *Dangerous When Wet: A Memoir of Booze, Sex, and My Mother* (St. Martin's Press), which was an Amazon "Best Book of May 2015," a Book Chase "2015 Nonfiction Top 10," and named "Required Reading" in Mary Karr's *The Art of Memoir*. His essays and articles have been published in the *New York Times, International Herald Tribune, Washington Post, Daily Beast, Salon*, and *Huffington Post*. A comedic storyteller, Brickhouse is the writer and performer of two award-winning solo shows *Dangerous When Wet* (based on his memoir) and *I Favor My Daddy* (based on his forthcoming memoir). He has recorded voices on *Beavis and Butthead*, appeared on The Moth Podcast, PBS-TV's *Stories from the Stage*, a National Storytelling Network Grand Slam winner, and is a four-time Moth StorySLAM champion. Brickhouse grew up in Beaumont, Texas, and graduated from Trinity University and the Radcliffe Publishing Course (now the Columbia Publishing Course). He lives with his common-law husband, Michael, in New York City.

Drae Campbell (she/her) performs all over NYC and on the internet and beyond. She's been spotted on IFC.com, *Conan*, Refinery29, and numerous films. Some acting credits: *Only You Can Prevent Wildfires,* Ricochet Collective, *Non-Consensual Relationships With Ghosts,* La Mama, *My Old Man*, Dixon Place, *Oph3lia* at HERE, *The Nosebleed* at The Public Theatre. On screen (large and small): *Dinette* and *Senior Escort Service* both directed by the great Shaina Feinberg, *New Amsterdam, Gay's Anatomy, Java, Evolved,* to name a few. Also Drae hosts and curates a live monthly show called TELL, a queer storytelling show that happens at The Bureau of General Services Queer Division and is now a Podcast on BRICRadio.

Calvin S. Cato (he/him) is a stand-up comedian, writer, and actor. His television appearances include the Game Show Network, Oxygen's *My Crazy Love*, National Geographic's *Brain Games*, and an unaired pilot for Vice Media called *Emergency Black Meeting.* His comedy has been featured in San Francisco Sketchfest, Austin's Out of Bounds Comedy

Festival, Brooklyn Pride, and the Women in Comedy Festival. In addition, his live storytelling has been featured on Keith and The Girl, RISK!, and Tinder Tales. In 2017, Calvin was named one of Time Out New York's Queer Comics of Color to Watch Out For.

Timothy Dunn (he/him) is some rich and debonair bon vivant, living in some skyscraper in New York City, where the wind barely ever manages to ruffle his perfectly-coiffed hair. Tim was a company member at the famed comedy theatre, The Upright Citizens Brigade Theatre, in New York City for over a decade, where he wrote, performed, and directed sketch comedy and hosted UCB's first queer comedy variety show, Queerball. Tim no longer dates boozers, users, or losers, and his dog, #TinyTacoParty, has never been happier.

Micheal Foulk (they/them) is an aggressively cute and friendly, non-binary queer comedian, writer, and educator from Austin, Texas who is now thriving in Oakland, California. Micheal is the co-creator of the LGBTQ+ storytelling show Greetings, from Queer Mountain and the creator/host of film screening series Queer Film Theory 101 produced in collaboration with Alamo Drafthouse Cinemas. Micheal has performed at festivals all over the country including SF Sketchfest, Out Of Bounds Comedy Festival, and Crom Comedy Fest and their essays have been featured in Slate, Vice, TimeOUT NYC, and Intomore. Micheal is currently writing two books, *This Is How They Get You*, a collection of non-fiction essays about the pitfalls and failures in navigating gender and sexuality in America, and *KANSAS*, a speculative fiction short story collection focused on the Great Plains throughout both the past and future.

Veronica Garza (she/her/baller) is a Brooklyn-based stand-up comedian who is originally from Dallas. She performs all over New York City and beyond. Veronica's been featured on MTV's *Decoded*, NPR, Sirius XM, and Daily Mail.

Christian Luu (they/them) is a nonbinary Vietnamese writer and performer based in Brooklyn, NY. They're originally from Dallas, Texas, and received a Bachelor of Music in Musical Theatre from the University of Central Oklahoma. Performance credits include Off-Broadway, Lincoln Center, HERE Arts Center, and more. You can see them writing for Reductress, Awf Magazine, and Overstep Comedy.

Philip Markle (he/him) has performed and produced in hundreds of shows and taught students internationally, from Berlin to Bali. Philip graduated from Northwestern University and trained as a comedian in Chicago at The Annoyance, iO, and Second City. He moved to NYC in 2013 to launch the theatre and training center of The Annoyance Theater NY, where he acted as its Executive Director until Fall 2016. He is now the Founder and Artistic Director of The Brooklyn Comedy Collective, where he currently teaches and performs. As a storyteller, he has performed at The Moth and The Paper Machete and is a writer on Medium.com with 100k+ reads. Philip released his first album of sixteen comedy songs in 2019 called *AT THE GAY BATHHOUSE* on streaming and digital platforms everywhere.

Jeffrey Marx (he/him) trained and performed at Upright Citizen's Brigade Theater from 2003-2016 where his live stage show became a podcast called "The Q: A Queer Talk Show." After appearing on ABC's *Glass House*, he began working behind the scenes as a casting producer for reality-TV and unscripted series including *MTVs The Real World*, *Project Runway, Nailed It!*, and the Emmy-nominated *We're Here* on HBO.

Danny Murphy (he/him) is a comedian, writer, and host based in New York. He is currently a co-host of one of the top podcasts for Betches Media, *Not Another True Crime Podcast*, and is also a weekly pop culture correspondent for SiriusXM's *Bennington Show* where he hosts a segment breaking down what is going on in the world of celebrities and beyond. On top of that, he hosts and produces a monthly variety show at Union Hall called *PASS THE AUX: A Deep Dive Into A Diva*. His writing has appeared in Marie Claire, Betches, Town & Country, Seventeen Magazine, and more.

David Odyssey (he/him) is a writer and performer living in Brooklyn, NY. He traces the mythic currents of contemporary queer life through his podcast *The Luminaries*, and previously for publications like *DAZED*, *Time Out New York*, and *Vulture*. In 2020, he performed his solo show REBIRTH! at The Duplex cabaret theater.

David Perez (he/him) is a Brooklyn-based writer/performer. His writing has appeared in The Rumpus, The Racket, and Contagious Magazine. His work has been seen at Steppenwolf Theatre, UCB, Dixon Place, Joe's Pub, and The Exponential Festival. In 2010, he was the center of a popular internet experiment called David on Demand where for seven days everything he did was controlled by tweets. It was great and also super terrible, and he has a bad tattoo to prove it. He is a proud graduate of Cornish College of the Arts.

Lorena Russi (she/her) is a queer, Latina, pro soccer player turned comedian and filmmaker. Her 10-year background in entertainment ranges from head writing for Spotify's "Game Plan" to working on *The Late Show w/ Stephen Colbert*. Her bilingual dad jokes have been featured on PBS, The New York Times, and Will Smith's Snapchat.

Kelli Trapnell (she/her/they/them) is a bisexual fiction writer whose work straddles the line between horror and the literary. She's a 2018 NYSCA/NYFA Artist Fellow in Fiction from The New York Foundation for the Arts. Her work has been featured in *Gigantic Sequins*, *Paper Darts*, *Motherboard*, and on the *Tales to Terrify* podcast, as well as live on the radio for WKCR. She has been a panelist at Clexacon, has worked for *The New Yorker* and is a regular script writer for Frederator Networks and contributor to *Albuquerque the Magazine*. Originally from Houston, Texas, she now lives in New Mexico with her cat and her fiancée, where she is hard at work on her first novel.

Dubbs Weinblatt (they/them) is the Founder and Executive Producer of Thank You For Coming Out, a queer improv show and now weekly podcast, and Co-Founder and Executive Producer of Craft Your Truth, an organization that encourages LGBTQ folks to use any kind of performance art as a way to express their stories and connect with their community around them. Dubbs brings their flair for performance, partnerships, and engagement to their role as the Associate Director of Education and Training at Keshet, a national organization that works for the full equality of all LGBTQ Jews and our families in Jewish life. Dubbs earned their B.S. from The Ohio State University and volunteers with New Alternatives. They are currently "writing a book" (also known as having a Google doc with a lot of ideas in it).

Zach Zimmerman (he/him) is a comedian and writer in Brooklyn. His album *Clean Comedy* debuted on the Billboard Top 10, and he's written for *The New Yorker*, *McSweeney's*, *The Washington Post,* and other outlets. At the time of writing, he has caught up on 11 seasons of *RuPaul's Drag Race* and *All-Stars.*

About Immigration Equality

Immigration Equality is the nation's leading LGBTQ immigrant rights organization. Since its founding, the organization has worked to secure safe haven, freedom to live openly, and equality for individuals and families in their community. Through direct legal services, policy advocacy, and impact litigation, Immigration Equality advocates for immigrants and families facing discrimination based on their sexual orientation, gender identity, or HIV status. Learn more at immigrationequality.com.

*A portion of proceeds from every book sale
go to support Immigration Equality.*

We thank you for your purchase.